Hold for Release

Heidi Glick

Cover Art by *Nicola Martinez*

White Rose Publishing, a division of Pelican Ventures, LLC
www.pelicanbookgroup.com PO Box 1738 *Aztec, NM * 87410
White Rose Publishing Circle and Rosebud logo is a trademark of Pelican Ventures, LLC
Publishing History
First Harbourlight Edition, 2023
Paperback Edition ISBN 978-1-5223-0415-9
Electronic Edition ISBN 978-1-5223-0414-2
Published in the United States of America

Dedication

I would like to dedicate this book to my mother, Elizabeth Mountz. When I was a child, my mom taught me to go back and revise my work and to do my best. I'd like to thank her for her love and support.

I'd also like to thank God; my husband (John Glick); Pelican Book Group; my BSF group; my ACFW Scribes critique partners; my beta readers (Laura Spelliscy and Jeffrey Reynolds); my sensitivity reader (Jessy Alvarado); the Cops and Writers forum on Facebook; fellow author and retired nurse, Marcy Dyer, and retired nurse, Melissa Gauvin; and fellow author, historian, and retired police officer, Wesley Harris. All mistakes are my own.

1

"Looking diligently lest any man fail of the grace of God; lest any root of bitterness springing up trouble you, and thereby many be defiled;" Hebrews 12:15, KJV

A scream escaped Carlotta Hartman's lips as the overhead light revealed its hidden secret.

Red everywhere.

So much blood.

Chills swept down Carlotta's spine as she inched closer to the lifeless creature lying nearby on the animal shelter floor. The worn, green linoleum provided a stark contrast to the surrounding crimson liquid. She swiped at the trickle on her face. She hadn't even realized tears were running down her cheeks. The poor dog.

After locking the front door behind her, Carlotta crept along the dim-lit hall, rounded the corner, and entered the supply room at the end of the hallway. She clasped a hand over her mouth. Six dead dogs. All lying in their own blood. Were there others?

Horrible things happened in the Queen City—or in those romantic suspense novels she kept at her day job on the shelves at the Hyde Park Branch of the Cincinnati Public Library—but never to her. Sure, awful things happened. Her husband, Jake, even reported on them. They just never happened to the two of them.

Carlotta wiped sweat beads off her neck and then crouched to inspect each corpse. Throats all slit. At least they'd died quick. She wiped a hand across her face, as tears poured down.

Dogs barked in the distance.

She jumped up, crouched in a defensive stance, and scanned the room for a potential weapon. A bright orange cell phone lay on the floor of the adjoining area. Not *any* device—*Ed's*. Her stomach churned.

Scissors glinted on the nearest counter. She snatched them and turned the blades outward. Smoke assaulted her nostrils, and she followed the scent. A flick of the switch and light illuminated Ed Gorman's darkened office. A fire raged in the metal trashcan.

"Ed?" After locking the door to his office, Carlotta inched closer.

A blue t-shirt and khaki shorts adorned the lifeless form on the floor behind the desk, a wrinkled issue of the local newspaper atop his chest. She set it aside and then sneaked closer to verify the body as Ed's.

He lay still. Burnt papers, a half-burnt flag with a peace sign on it, and a shattered dove figurine were heaped in a metal wastebasket two feet from the body. Why had someone done this, and how had they gotten in? It was like some dark tale told by Uncle Ramon to amuse her and her siblings. Only this wasn't meant to entertain.

Discarding the scissors, Carlotta searched for her

boss's pulse. Nonexistent. She leaned closer. No knife wounds on his body. "Ed, are you OK?" Using clammy hands, she shook him. Her heart was slowing into heavy beats that made her sluggish. Terror gripped her insides. But she needed to help him. It took every ounce of will to shake him again. No response. Bending down near his mouth, she listened for breaths and counted. Ten. Eight. Four. One.

No gasping, no breathing at all.

Carlotta dialed 9-1-1.

"Nine-one-one. What is your emergency?"

"Um. I'm at the animal shelter on Madison Road. And someone..." Carlotta choked back a sob. "Some lowlife hurt the volunteer coordinator and killed several dogs. I locked the front door of the animal shelter."

"Is there anyone else there with you?"

"Just the coordinator. He's unresponsive. I'm starting CPR."

Carlotta put her phone on speaker and set it on the floor. She positioned herself to one side of Ed's body and placed her right hand on his chest, followed by her left hand on top. Kneeling forward and leveraging her body weight, she administered compressions. One. Two. Ten. Fifteen. Twenty. Thirty.

"The police will arrive soon," the operator said. "I'll stay on the line with you."

"Thank you." Carlotta tilted Ed's head back, pinched his nose shut, and then delivered one breath. His chest didn't rise. After checking to ensure his head was tilted adequately, she delivered another breath and clenched her fists. *C'mon, Ed.*

Repositioning her hands on his chest, Carlotta started more compressions. One. Two. Thirty. She checked his mouth. No obstructions. She continued to breathe. Still nothing.

Carlotta slammed her fist on the floor. Why didn't they have an AED device?

She kept compressing. More rescue breaths. Nothing. Carlotta continued compressions. Then she administered two rescue breaths. Back to compressions. Fifth cycle. Then what? Two rescue breaths. Pain shot through her arm muscles, and she sobbed. Five cycles of CPR. No movement, no sounds from Ed.

She felt her arm and then touched him again.

He's cold. Ed's gone. He's really gone. She cradled her head in her hands and sobbed. *I can't help him anymore. What if I'm in danger?* "The v...volunteer co...coordinator is dead." Carlotta's words were shaky as she touched her arm again and then Ed's to confirm. "I've tried CPR, but he's very cold to the touch. Obviously, uh," her voice cracked, "dead."

"OK, ma'am. You tried your best, but I'm concerned about your safety. The police will arrive soon, but I'd like you to try to get outside. The intruder could still be on the premises."

"Uh-uh. I'm locked in an office. I feel safe in here." Her breaths became ragged. She wrapped her hands around her knees and rocked back and forth. "I'm not doing it. Sorry."

"OK, ma'am. But I would feel better if you went

outside."

Carlotta shifted her attention to the cabinets in Ed's office. The intruder had broken locks and opened cabinet doors. Supplies littered the floor along with a piece of gauze and a syringe. Had someone killed Ed to get drugs? A month prior, Jake had reported on a burglary at the pharmacy down the street. Memories of her own brother-in-law's desperation to score heroin flooded her mind. Addicts rarely cared who they hurt, including themselves. Like with Mom and her drinking problem.

The dogs resumed barking.

She sighed. Alone and surrounded by the stench of death and stale air until help arrived.

"I heard a noise. Is everything OK, ma'am?"

"Yes." Maybe not totally alone. But what good could the operator do if the intruder was still nearby? She peered through the glass window at the top of Ed's office door. The faulty light fixture at the other end of the building flickered. Her chest pounded harder. Carlotta shook her head. Not a panic attack. Not here, not now.

"Are you sure you're OK, ma'am?"

"Yes, I...I need...to...take some deep breaths. I'll be fine."

Fine. Her standard response to everything in life, even when it wasn't. Carlotta inhaled deep breaths as she'd learned in an article during her lunch break at the library. She shoved back childhood memories threatening to surface. Her mind grew foggy. Carlotta scrunched her eyes shut. *Think.* She opened them.

Maybe she should listen to the operator and run outside. What if he broke through Ed's office door? He *or* she. Jake always reminded her not to assume a suspect's gender.

Carlotta shifted her gaze to the other side of Ed's room. The private bathroom. She'd forgotten about it. It adjoined with Ed's office. As she crept closer, the scent of citrus bathroom cleaner became evident. What if she locked herself inside with the intruder?

Ugh. The only room with the light switch behind the door. Using her cell phone display, she provided herself with just enough light. What if the killer noticed it, too? As she prowled closer, goosebumps swept over her. Carlotta tripped over her foot, stumbled for the light switch, and flipped it on. She wandered around the room. Nothing out of the ordinary. She slumped against the wall. Her shoulders relaxed.

A cacophony of barks sounded in the distance, and her stomach danced. Carlotta fidgeted with the gold cross on the chain around her neck. It'd been a while since she'd stepped inside a church or talked to God. Would He listen to her now?

Jake had prayed for his dad to live. Clearly, that hadn't turned out. Who was to say God would protect her? Where was He during the huge thunderstorm when she was little? She swiped a tear and shook her head.

If only Jake were around to protect her. She'd melt into his arms. They'd had some arguments as of late, but once she got out of there...no way she could be angry with him.

~*~

Jake Hartman sat at his desk and played with his gold wedding band. An image of his fiery, petite brunette wife flashed through his mind. How mad would Carlotta be once he saw her later that evening?

Jake repositioned a framed photo of an article about journalist Victor Riesel on his desk to reveal the rose bouquet behind it. Leaning in closer, he took in the floral, fragrant smell and then grabbed the bouquet. After lifting the flowers, ready to toss them in the trash, he set them back down and covered his face with his hands. What was he thinking? As if flowers would compensate for his wrong. He shifted good ole' Victor's photo in front of the roses.

Jake's shoulders tightened. Poor Victor. Having a gangster exact retribution on him. Revenge. What an ugly thing. It happened to journalists sometimes— being hurt or killed. Shaking his head, Jake shifted his gaze back to the flowers.

He sighed. The bouquet wouldn't make up for his mess. Got to start somewhere. Jake rubbed his neck. Maybe two dozen flowers would have been better. At least he had time to stop off at the florist's shop on his way back from interviewing the mayor. Not his most exciting interview as a journalist, but more desirable than writing recipes for the food section of the newspaper. At least Stu tossed most of the crime reporting gigs his way. They were the assignments bosses often gave to the newbies, yet Jake found a thrill in them. Not the crimes themselves. But wondering what made someone tick, what set them off. And of course, there were the victims. He wanted to write about them with dignity. Could a reporter straight out of college do as good of a job as he could?

As a journalist, he was driven by a need to uncover the truth. Still, over the years, compassion fatigue set in. How many tragedies could he get worked up over? But people talked to him. He had a way of getting them to open up. Otherwise, Stu might overlook him for some of the younger employees. And yet, by now, he hoped to be higher up the rungs on the career ladder, closer to senior editor.

No, his career wasn't turning out as planned. A lot like his marriage. Jake cracked his knuckles. Was it wrong to want a pleasant, peaceful evening where Carlotta would eventually forget everything? He huffed. As if that would happen. Regardless of what he wanted, what happened with Allison was like a breaking story begging to be told. The truth needed to come out. If only he knew what the truth was. Jake rubbed his eyes, trying to remember.

He'd had a drink or two. He didn't remember being drunk, but he couldn't recall much else, either. Maybe it was a blessing that he couldn't. *Not that Carlotta will believe me.* Even donning a scarlet letter might not appease her.

He curled his hands inward. His mind raced to the past. As a young man, he'd squirmed next to Granny on a hard wooden church pew. From the pulpit, the loud, fiery preacher yelled a slew of acrid remarks about various topics. The Big A happened to be one of them. If Jake took as much stock in God as Granny did, that might be a conundrum. But he'd graduated to other ways of thinking. Not that the God stuff was all bad. Loving your neighbor, being nice. Some of it was helpful. Like any article, Jake edited out the bad, kept the good. Whatever worked with his philosophy of life.

As for Carlotta, all he could offer her about the night in question was what he could remember. Then, and only then, could the two of them move forward, get past this. Speaking of things to fix…

Shifting his focus to his work assignment, Jake killed the last section of his story on the current Cincinnati mayor, rewrote and saved it, and shut down the computer. He located his to-do list and crossed off his last item. Good thing Carlotta had suggested creating one.

With Stu close to retirement, a handful of news pieces like this latest, and Jake would replace his boss as senior editor and gain more control over his assignments. Half the time, Stu took credit for his story ideas. He stole a glance at his boss across the office. If only he could speak up. Nope. Better to bide his time than to lose his chance at his dream job. Besides, while he was an accomplished news journalist, he'd made his share of mistakes.

But his actual goal—how badly he wanted it— Carlotta wouldn't understand or care. For years, she'd helped him stay on task, avoid procrastination, and keep track of things. These days, he could drop dead, and she probably wouldn't notice. Only one thing on her mind, and it wasn't him. And presumably not fun, excitement, or adventure, either.

He opened his top left drawer and sifted through it. A paper tumbled out, and he stuffed it back inside. Jake opened the right desk drawer and, after rifling through another pile of papers, located a flyer for an upcoming escape room game in Hyde Park. He set the crumpled pamphlet next to his computer. While he would have more fun zip lining, or kayaking, Carlotta would prefer escape rooms and murder mystery dinners. Before visions of babies had clouded Carlotta's thinking, they could have fun together. The plotting of menstrual cycles, infertility drugs, and trips to the doctor's office had replaced movies, dinner dates, and long walks. Nothing wrong with wanting a baby, but… Carlotta's hopes and dreams had become an obsession.

Jake's cell vibrated, and he leaned back in his office chair. He glanced at the display. An incoming text from Carlotta.

You've got to get over here. Fast.

Carlotta's message sounded frantic. Yikes, something sure flipped her lid. Like how Mom acted anytime Jake would get sick after Dad had died. Cancer changed lives, and not only the person whose life it claimed. Nope, it ate through everyone. Like his faith. God was supposed to be benevolent, but He allowed good people to die.

The phone chimed. Another text from his wife.

Are you working on a story?

So what was the crisis this time? Another failed pregnancy test? Hadn't she checked last week? Jake focused on the bouquet. Perhaps he should have opted for a puppy instead, attempted to quell her mothering time clock. Adoption wasn't an option. He shook his head. Don't even get him started on her family. Uh-uh. Maybe he could encourage Carlotta to join a women's group at the church around the corner. Too religious for his taste. Still, the men's group had helped him gain some work connections. Not a total waste of time. Jake held his phone and slid one foot at a time back into his loafers. He texted a response.

What is it, baby? Carlotta, R U OK?

Jake's jaw tightened. Had she already found out? Who else would even know?

6 dogs killed.

They didn't own any... oh, *those* dogs, at the animal shelter. Sorry, but they couldn't keep them all. She was always wanting to take in some lost cause. He scratched his head. Like him.

6 are dead.

Bad dog kibble? He responded.

Like the story he'd covered three years ago. Probably another case of cheap, tainted dog chow from Asia.

U sound upset. Have you been taking more of those hormones?

She could be jumpy, especially lately. Like a smoke alarm going off for no reason.

Ed is dead. Thought you'd want a scoop on the story. I'm on the phone with 9-1-1.

A knot formed in the pit of his stomach.

B there soon. B careful.

Delicate hands massaged Jake's shoulders, and their owner let out a sigh. Hands covered his eyes. A sickening, yet familiar, scent of lemons overpowered his senses. Jake spun his office chair around. Buxom-blonde Allison in a tight, hot pink suit. All five feet, ten inches, and one hundred and twenty pounds of her. Jake's cheeks flamed at the knowledge. One time this journalist did not want the facts. Was it his imagination, or had she become more aggressive? Or had he been so desperate to talk to someone else, he'd overlooked obvious warning signs?

That night, Allison had said she wanted advice on an assignment. Not that many years ago, Jake had been the newbie. He knew what it was like. He'd just wanted to help. And then, like any talented journalist, she got him to talk. Yeah, he should have discussed his problems with Carlotta and not with Allison. But Carlotta had been volunteering more and more lately. She didn't have time for him, and that night, Allison did. The alcohol didn't help matters.

"I've been looking all over for you," Allison said.

"I… I interviewed the mayor earlier." Jake stood, averted his gaze, and moved out of her way. "I've gotta go."

Allison blocked Jake's path and grabbed his shoulders. "What is it, sweetie? The wife?"

He quirked a brow. *Why did I ever talk with her?*

"You and I should go out again for drinks," she said. "We could just talk."

Yeah, like last time. No, thanks. Jake pried off Allison's brightly painted claws, put on his sport coat and black fedora, grabbed his car keys, and dashed down the hall. "A dead man and dogs at the shelter. Carlotta's shaken up." He bit his lip. "She could be in danger." Carlotta just had to be there alone. Who volunteered at night after work? And for a nonprofit, no less. Only Carlotta, the do-gooder. Anything to help her stay busy and keep her from dealing with reality.

A tall, dark-haired, hefty figure stepped closer and stopped short of colliding with him. "Whoa."

The kid from the entertainment section. Todd, No. Keith? Randy, Randy Rader. Likable guy, but somewhat green. Jake performed a double take at Randy's attire—a black shirt with a blue telephone booth and black and blue plaid pants. Apparently, the guy enjoyed watching a certain British science fiction show. Come to think of it, he'd like a time machine himself, so he could go back and avoid spending time with Allison in the first place.

"Oops. My bad." Randy adjusted his glasses. "Hey, did you say dead animals? Where and when?"

"My wife volunteers at the McKinley Animal Shelter. Dogs were killed, also, the director." He pushed past the kid, raced toward the lone elevator, and pressed the lit green arrow.

When the elevator doors opened, Randy tripped as he followed Jake inside and shook his head. "The triad, dude. The McDonald Triad." Hydraulics pressed the elevator doors shut. The shaft creaked.

Jake rubbed his temple. "Huh?" The lingering odor of a variety of hygiene products worn by other employees overwhelmed him.

Randy counted off on his fingers. "You know, bedwetting, fire-setting, animal cruelty. Three characteristics that can predict psychopathic behavior."

Jake loosened the blue tie Carlotta had given him for his last birthday and examined it. "Yeah, I'm familiar with the triad. What does that have to do with this?"

"We've received several reports of arson fires lately. Shelly's on maternity leave. So, I'm working on a story right now. Now those animals at the shelter..."

Bing. The elevator stopped, and the doors opened. Jake stepped forward, teetering on his right foot. One more step and he'd hit the mail guy—tall kid, dark hair, yellow jogging suit—like a giant pencil. Wow, could Pencil Boy's cart be any fuller? After the cart passed, Jake hopped out and darted toward the front door of the *Cincinnati News* building, but then he stopped and oscillated toward his coworker. "What, no number three for your triad, man?"

Randy exited the elevator and shrugged.

Jake stepped closer and patted Randy on the shoulder. "As my math teacher used to say, 'Keep this to yourself.'" He shifted his gaze upward. "And get some new pants. If there is one thing Stu doesn't trust—"

Randy grimaced. "People who speak with accents—"

Jake counted off on his fingers. "Wear plaid, mispronounce names... I gotta go." He hurried outside, his path illuminated by muted lights overhead. He unlocked and opened the door to his shiny red compact car, climbed inside. and fastened his seat belt. Jake started the car engine and kicked off his brown loafers. Much improved. He grabbed his cell phone and texted Carlotta. *I'm on my way.*

Dogs R barking again. I think someone might B outside.

Maybe it's the police, baby. Any sign of them yet? Ask the 9-1-1 operator. His phone alarm chimed. A reminder to pick up Carlotta for dinner. Perhaps Jake should tell her his news at the animal shelter and not at the restaurant. Might be handy to have some officers on hand, keep the peace.

No. And I smell smoke 2. wondering if I should leave. I better tell the operator.

Arson. Dead animals. Jake dropped his phone. He blew out a breath, muttered a curse, and threw the vehicle in reverse. His wheels screeched as he drove across rows of empty parking spaces and raced out of the parking lot. "Whatever you do, Carly, don't become my next exclusive. I don't want to report on you."

2

A distant siren sounded, followed by a rap at the front door of the animal shelter. Carlotta's heart pounded faster than Papi's hands could play the *congas*. If only Jake was here. What would he say?

Her mind flashed to memories of all the suspense novels she'd read while waiting for Jake to get home from work. Could she obtain some sort of advice for this situation?

Another knock. What killer knocked on the door? Carlotta unlocked the door of Ed's office and crept toward the entryway. The police had wasted no time in getting here.

"They're here. Thanks," she mumbled into her phone. She turned it off and stuffed it in her pocket. Minutes earlier, the operator had let her know the police were almost there. Must have been them.

Carlotta hesitated before unlocking the dead bolt and slowly unlatching the old chain lock Ed had installed. She blinked rapidly. Ed had worked at the shelter for as long as she'd been a volunteer. How could he be dead?

She reached for the doorknob but refused to turn it. Carlotta drew in a shaky breath. What if it wasn't the police? The siren from earlier had ended. She blew out another breath. Who else would it be? They probably turned off the siren as they got closer.

Wham. A thud against the window. A younger-looking man pressed his face against the glass, wild eyes peering directly at her. Carlotta screamed.

The man rapped on the windowpane. "Are you OK in there? Are you hurt?" He flung open the unlocked door and approached—still maintaining a fair distance between them. A familiar scent accompanied him—like her *abuelo* after smoking a pipe. "I started working in the building next door recently. I thought I heard a scream." Dirty-blond hair and glasses framed his slender face. He wore a mint green polo shirt, khaki slacks, and brown dress shoes— overdressed compared to her pink blouse, khaki skort, and white tennies. Definitely younger than her, by maybe five years or more. Very early thirties, perhaps?

She looked away from his intrusive stare. "That was me. I'm so scared."

"Are you all right?"

"I am, but someone broke in here. My boss and, um, several dogs are dead. The intruder stole some items and started a fire. I already called the police. They should be here soon." She clasped one hand to her chest. "Sorry. You scared me at first."

"Are you sure you're OK?"

She looked up to meet his gaze. "Yes, I'm fine." *Fine.* That word again. Carlotta took a deep breath. "I'm glad you're here. Would you mind staying with me until the police arrive?"

A slight smile spread across the man's face.

"Certainly."

Carlotta unwrapped a stick of gum, popped it in her mouth, and chomped it like a pack of Chihuahuas attacking a calf's ankle—something her uncle had claimed to have witnessed firsthand though she doubted the veracity of his claim. If he were still alive, oh, what a story she'd have to share.

A spider scurried across the floor. Eek! Carlotta stomped it with her shoe. "I don't like bugs."

"You are not alone. Entomophobia is a common fear."

Not alone, eh? *I'm a bug freak, and there are more of us.* Great.

A minute later, a Cincinnati PD cruiser pulled into the driveway, and Carlotta pointed. "There they are." She turned to Wild Eyes and reached out to shake his hand. "Thank you for checking in, Mr...."

"Mr. Walters, with Walters and Petersheim. It's the law firm in the brownstone next door." He handed her his card and pointed to the phone number. "If you need anything, please call."

Carlotta nodded.

An officer approached and identified himself as Officer King—a very tall man with blond hair and blue eyes.

As Carlotta provided her name to the police officer, Mr. Walters disappeared. Carlotta started to toss the card into the trash but then stuffed it in her pocket. The man didn't say what kind of law he practiced. Maybe he handled adoptions. Better to keep his card, just in case. As a last resort. No one said she had to like Jake's idea of adopting children instead of undergoing more infertility treatments. But even she had to admit the current plan was getting them nowhere.

"Step outside." Officer King stood with his gun ready and entered the animal shelter building just as she'd seen police do on crime shows on TV. Except this was real life. Her life.

The man returned. "I've checked all the rooms. There's no one else inside." He went over to his vehicle and removed a clipboard. "How are you?"

"Fine." She willed her hands to stop shaking.

"When did you get here?"

"Uh, around 6:00 PM." She swallowed hard and answered more questions from the officer.

Jake arrived in a slightly wrinkled dress shirt, sport coat, khakis, and hat and jogged over to them.

The officer studied Jake and his bare feet. The officer didn't know Jake liked to drive barefoot. It was one of the quirks she'd loved about him. Once. Now, it just irked her. Would it kill Jake to wear some shoes in public?

Carlotta raised her hand. "It's OK. He's my husband. I called him after I found the dogs and then Ed, uh, Mr. Gorman."

The officer stepped toward Jake. "I'm sorry, sir, but I need..."

An athletic blonde, and a tall man with dark hair and kind eyes joined them.

Officer King stepped toward the female. "Detective Krouse." He handed her a clipboard.

Krouse nodded at King. "It's OK. Detective Hadley and I will handle the scene from here. For now, you can patrol the perimeter." The detective wrote on the paper, and then Officer King walked away.

"Thank you." Jake stepped forward.

"Uh-uh," Krouse scolded and tugged on latex gloves. "Sorry, Jake. Today, you get to be a statue. Stay right there."

So the blonde was on a first-name basis with Carlotta's husband. Jake did report on a lot that happened in the city; it only made sense. Perhaps her little tinge of jealousy was misplaced. Nevertheless, it bubbled inside. What else didn't she know about her husband?

"Reporters," Hadley huffed and then put on some gloves, too.

As the detectives entered the building, an image of the dead dogs flashed in Carlotta's mind. If it weren't for the fact she had spent time with the poor creatures, she wouldn't have been able to recognize them. What sort of monster did something like this? Her chin trembled. She put a hand to her forehead. "What if I hadn't hit all those red lights on the way here? What if I'd arrived minutes earlier?"

Jake put his hands on her shoulders and looked her in the eyes. "You can't go there, baby."

She shivered.

Leaning closer, Jake wrapped his arms around her. "It'll be OK."

Carlotta relaxed in her husband's embrace, something she hadn't done much of lately.

Minutes later, Detectives Hadley and Krouse walked back outside.

"I'll need names of everyone who has access to this building."

Hadley handed her a pen and paper.

"Sure." Stepping away, Carlotta wrote the names of the owner and other volunteers. She showed the list to the officer and pointed to the one at the top. "Ed Gorman, the victim, owns the facility. I volunteer here."

"And you're here at night, alone?" Hadley raised a brow.

Jake shook his head. "I've been saying the same thing for years."

Carlotta cleared her throat and scooted next to Jake. "I volunteer here some evenings and weekends, but some animals get lonely at night. I like to check on them, especially the new ones." That and it helped her forget her own pain. Her sister, sisters-in-law, and cousins could churn out children faster than a *jai alai* ball being hurled from a *cesta*, and she couldn't even give birth to one.

Jake wrapped his arm around her.

"Did the shelter have any enemies?" Krouse asked. "Receive any hate mail?"

"Hate mail? No. Everyone liked Ed." Especially her sister. How would Rosario take the news?

Jake raised an index finger. "Not everyone."

If looks could kill, Jake ought to be ten feet under from her stare.

Jake shrugged and stared at Carlotta. "What?" He

faced Krouse. "Carlotta's estranged brother-in-law, Pablo Martinez, served in the Army. Drug addict. After her sister separated from Pablo, he caught her having coffee with Ed. They were just being friendly, but Pablo got jealous."

Carlotta gasped. Then again, he was telling the truth. *I shouldn't be so hard on him. He's only trying to help.*

"Pablo thought of Ed as a hippie, the draft dodger-type."

The burnt flag in Ed's office. Could Pablo have done this?

Krouse cleared her throat and shifted closer to Jake. "What about that group? Um, Jake, who were the activists you reported on last year?"

"The APCC, Animal Protection Confederation of Cincinnati. Yeah, they frown on no-kills."

Carlotta rubbed her chin. "Wait. Ed received a letter in the mail the other day. He seemed upset about it. It might be on his desk."

Krouse jogged back inside the building and returned with an envelope.

"Do you keep cash on the premises?" Hadley asked. "I saw a broken lockbox."

"We keep medicines in there," Carlotta said.

"What sort of medications?"

"Sedatives, painkillers...oh, and hypodermic needles." The shelter was already under-funded and with Ed dead, could it recover from such a mess? She could offer to volunteer more of her time. And maybe she could convince Jake to donate to the shelter, foster a few animals to help to defray costs, or pen a human-interest story to help raise awareness. Surely, they could help more in some way.

Hadley rubbed his chin. "Cash and drugs. Those are solid motives. You may leave now, ma'am. We'll contact you later if needed."

Carlotta went to her car. She could discuss her ideas to help the animal shelter over dinner.

Jake opened his mouth and then stopped short.

"What is it?"

"This kid at work. He lives for conspiracy theories. This will get him all fired up about the triad. I'll have to hear about it for days." Jake rolled his eyes.

"The triad?"

Jake positioned his arm around her, but she wiggled from his hold and stepped toward her car. "The McDonald Triad. It details three characteristics of psychopaths."

"What does that have to do with the animal shelter?"

"Nothing at all. Nice kid, but paranoid. Kind of like my Uncle Larry."

Carlotta pointed her key fob at her car.

His hand touched hers. "Leave your car here. We can get it tomorrow."

She followed him. "Why can't I drive it home?"

Jake opened her door. "Because we have dinner reservations."

Carlotta rubbed her arms. The temperature had dipped down a bit since earlier in the day. "Dinner? Tonight? Maybe we could call and order take out instead, considering all that just happened."

"We really need to…" Jake sighed and took a deep breath. "It's fine. We can go out later this week. I rented a movie from one of those machines. Picked up the romantic comedy you've been talking about for weeks. We can have a nice quiet evening, well, what's left of it, at least."

Carlotta trembled.

Jake removed his coat and wrapped it around her. But a coldness lingered, and it had nothing to do with the weather and more with the storm brewing in their relationship. He walked her to her car, like a parent leading a child. At times, a comforting gesture, at others times, controlling. But, that was just his way. He was a take charge kind of guy.

A furry object scurried under Jake's vehicle. "Meow."

"Did you see that?" Carlotta asked.

Jake nodded and bent down. "Gotcha."

"Meow."

Jake held a gray kitten and scratched its head. "Guess it's good we're not going out to eat. I'll stop at the corner store and grab some kitty food. Maybe later this week, you can take it to the animal shelter. Unless you want to keep it."

The shelter. Carlotta winced as she climbed in the car.

Jake removed his fedora, and placed the kitten inside the hat and then on Carlotta's lap.

She petted the creature.

As Jake drove away, the kitten settled down.

Carlotta shifted her gaze out the window, her brain on autopilot most of the way. When finally safe in her own home, Carlotta watered her house plants, starting with the ferns, Mary and Jane, and then she moved on to the spider plants, Lydia and Kitty. Finally, she approached Elizabeth, who sat near the sink. For some reason, the Christmas cactus wouldn't bloom. Strong arms wrapped around Carlotta's waist, and she jumped. She turned to face Jake.

"Sorry, I didn't mean to scare you."

Carlotta gestured to the cactus. "I can't take care of plants." She crossed her arms. "Perhaps you better feed the kitten."

Jake reached for Carlotta. "Maybe the cactus needs some better soil or fertilizer."

Carlotta pushed the plant toward the window. "Or more light."

Jake scrunched his nose. "Yeah, I'm not so sure about that." He moved the plant back to its original location. "My grandma used to say too much light can scorch them."

The kitten stumbled into the room and meowed, and Jake fed it.

"I need to take a bath." Carlotta walked away. She ran the water in the old clawfoot tub and added bubble bath. After several minutes, she checked the water temperature and climbed in. A lavender scent filled the room. Bubbles enveloping her, Carlotta lounged in her tub and stared at nothing in particular. *Poor Ed was really dead.* Her hands shook, and tears welled. She sobbed until her tears were spent. She'd need to tell her sister about his death. Carlotta didn't know if their casual dates had turned into something else for Rosario. At that consideration, the tears she'd thought she was done with cascaded again.

And because Ed was dead, she'd managed to avoid dinner with Jake for another night. She berated herself for the selfishness of that thought. But if they went out, they'd see happy couples with kids. Did God not think she was nurturing enough to be a mother? She'd had to bow out from volunteering to help with story time at the library to maintain her sanity. Moms and babies—just too much. Especially the teen moms—proof that anyone and everyone, except her, could get pregnant.

~*~

Had it only been a day since Ed's death? Sighing, Carlotta sank deep into her chair at the checkout desk and glanced at the clock. Five more minutes, and she could go home. Take another bubble bath. Forget what happened the day before.

A tall, brown-haired man in a red cap carrying a brown bag approached. He plunked a book on the counter and looked at her. His eyes widened. "Carlotta?"

Her gaze narrowed. He'd slimmed down. Lost a few pounds. Plus, she'd never seen him wear a hat to the library before.

"Xavier? Your card, please."

He leaned forward and handed her his card. A

pleasant, woodsy, manly cologne smell accompanied him.

She scanned the card and then returned it to him. "Thanks."

"I haven't seen you for a while, Carlotta." Xavier's gaze shifted downward. "I, I uh, went camping with some friends."

Maybe college buddies. From all appearances, he had to be younger than her. She picked up the book he'd set down. "*Catcher in the Rye*? You know, oddly enough, I've never read it." She scanned the book and set it aside.

"Neither have I. Oh, one more thing." Xavier reached into the bag slung over his shoulder and retrieved a DVD. He set it on the counter and slid it toward Carlotta.

Carlotta picked up the movie and scanned it. "*Zodiac*?"

He grinned and looked away. "Yeah, maybe you can recommend some other true crime stories for me."

She glanced at the back of the DVD and set it atop the book. "This would be right up my husband's alley."

"Oh, I didn't know you were married." Xavier shoved his hands in his pockets.

"Yeah. To a newspaper journalist."

How did he not know she was...? She glimpsed the fingers on her left hand where her rings had been. The fertility hormones had made her fingers swollen. So she'd taken them off lately. And maybe Xavier hadn't noticed.

"Huh." Xavier pulled at his collar.

Carlotta printed a receipt for Xavier. "I'm finished working the desk in about five minutes. When my replacement comes, I'd be happy to walk you over to the true crime section. Or you could ask the librarian at the reference desk."

"You know, I just remembered I have to, um, meet a buddy for dinner. Maybe I'll come back and check out more books and DVDs then."

"OK." She handed him the book and movie. "They're due back in two weeks. Bye."

Xavier waved and walked away.

Her coworker, Nicole, approached.

Carlotta quirked a brow. "You're here early."

"Not much traffic." Nicole folded her arms. "You let poor Xavier down easily, I hope."

"What do you mean?" Carlotta got up from her seat and moved aside.

Nicole plopped down onto the chair and shook her head. "C'mon. It's obvious that guy has a crush on you."

"Really? I never, well, now that you say it. Anyway, I told him I'm married, so now he knows." Even if he had feelings for her, it was just a little crush. Completely harmless. Not like the stalker in the romantic suspense book she'd put on hold. The back cover blurb made that guy sound like a psycho.

After the animal shelter break-in, Jake's coworker had mentioned some triad involving psychopaths. If there had been a psychopath on the loose...

Her phone chimed.

I made reservations for dinner tomorrow night.

She swept a hand across her forehead. He was trying to be nice. She needed to go and try to enjoy the evening.

~*~

Carlotta swiped her brow. What a day. But she'd survived. Always a relief after an author event. And this one was quite the diva. Demanding this and that. But it was over now. Even though the woman's acrid perfume scent still lingered.

Parents had picked up the unattended kids in the children's section, and Carlotta had re-shelved the books in the nonfiction section correctly. She held a book closer and sniffed the pages. The older the book, often, the better the smell. Sweet, like vanilla flowers and almonds. Given her chaotic home life, she'd found solace in books. Maybe that's why she became so defensive when patrons treated them carelessly.

After locating books to be put on hold, Carlotta placed them on a cart and wheeled them behind the front desk. She glanced at the library clock: 5:00 PM. No getting out of dinner tonight. *Forget how it makes you feel. Think of Jake.*

She went outside and sat on a bench to wait for Jake. She removed a historic fiction book from her purse and began reading. The clearing of a throat tore her gaze away from the World War II scene and to her husband, now standing several feet away. Carlotta stuffed the book back into her purse. The hero would have to rescue the heroine later. Her own hero, or was he a former hero now that they seemed to be falling apart, walked toward her. He moved with easy grace and had shoes on this time.

"I have to ask something." He gave her that smile she loved and then frowned a little.

When had they lost their place in their own lives? She leaned in and put her arms around his neck, unconsciously parting her lips. "As a journalist or as my husband?"

Moving closer, Jake put his hands on her waist. "Any unusual patrons at the library, babe?"

Carlotta released her hold with surprising reluctance. "Nicole thinks one has...*had* a crush on me."

Jake quirked a brow. "Had?"

Carlotta shrugged. "I told him I was married."

Her husband looked down at the ground and shuffled his feet. "What about Oliver?"

"Oliver Robertson? What about him?" She crossed her arms. "You don't think he...? C'mon, Jake. He's the pacifist type."

Jake frowned. "But I stole his fiancée. All bets are off." Jake rubbed his face. "Has a pretty good right hook if I remember correctly. What's he up to now?"

"Has some sort of Eco Tour experience near Dayton. Out in the country. Zip lining, kayaking, crossbows, archery, and everything. Recreated the ancient mound earthworks found throughout Ohio."

Jake pursed his lips. "Sounds as if you've been keeping tabs."

"Saw him in a magazine at the library. I read on my break sometimes. And while I read your articles, I also read about things other than crime."

He nodded and crossed his arms.

Carlotta's stomach quivered. She tried to slow her breathing.

Grabbing her hand, Jake asked. "Everything OK?"

"Yeah."

Sighing, Jake patted his coat. "Ugh."

"What is it?" Most likely he'd forgotten his wallet or watch. The usual suspects.

He threw his hands in the air. "The flowers. I left them at my desk."

"You bought flowers?" She recounted the other times he'd purchased them and winced.

"Yes, is that OK?"

"You only give me flowers when you've done something wrong." She studied his eyes. Like Dad after a late-night business meeting with his attractive secretary. Jake had been working later more often. At first, she relished the quiet time to finish novels she'd bring home from work. But then things became too silent. Who could she confide to about her infertility struggle? Certainly not Rosario. Nope, her sister wouldn't understand. She shouldn't let her mind run wild. Maybe he worked late to avoid the pain, too.

Jake avoided her gaze.

"When they examined Ed...did they find he'd been tortured, or something equally gruesome?" Carlotta could hardly stand the thought.

"Nooo..."

"Or is someone else we know pregnant?" Each announcement, another reminder of her failures. Carlotta swiped a tear and headed toward her car.

Her husband stopped her from opening the door. "What are you doing? Come with me."

"I don't want to."

He tugged her close. "I'm sorry about what happened to Ed. But you need to hear what I have to say. I've put it off for far too long. Waiting any longer will not make things better."

"Fine. But please, no mention of adoption. Not tonight." She followed him and hopped into his car—anything at this point to get her mind off of Ed's death and her own shortcomings. Life couldn't get much lower than this.

3

"You weren't working late on some project. You were..." Carlotta shifted her gaze to the crystal chandeliers dangling over the round restaurant tables where fellow patrons dined on filet and lobster, regained her composure, lowered her voice and scowled. "You know, with that woman from your office."

"Shh. As I said, it wasn't my intention, and it won't ever happen again. I only wanted someone to talk to. Things have been rough, Carlotta. Things have become..." He cleared his throat.

Carlotta glanced upward, ping-ponged her gaze back to Jake and away again. His woodsy cologne overwhelmed her, enticing and repulsing at the same time.

"Well, frankly, things have become mechanical. Less spontaneous. Infertility doctors have stepped in and taken over our love life. Are you even listening to me?"

Carlotta clenched her fists. Her nails bit into her palms. A vision of Jake's buxom coworker plagued her thoughts. *It won't happen again*? Exactly how many times had Jake committed adultery? Carlotta tugged on her stretchy pink top, pulling it over her expanding waistline. Was it her fault he'd strayed? All those pounds she'd gained while taking fertility drugs.

Her gaze shifted to the white votive candle in the center of the table. "You brought me here on purpose. So I couldn't make a scene. Controlling. That's what you are, Jake."

"C'mon, Carlotta. I'm a take charge kind of guy. That's what you've always liked about me." He reached for her hand, but she pulled it away. "Did like. Look. I know things have been rough with this infertility phase."

Her nostrils flared. "Is that all this is to you? A rough patch you hope we'll soon get over? Our life is not like one of your stories. You can't edit and revise it to improve it. It doesn't work that way." Yesterday, her sister had voiced concerns about Jake being too controlling. Carlotta hadn't agreed. Then. "Just yesterday," she said and then shook her head. "Never mind. This. Is. It. I've had it." She removed her linen napkin from her lap and tossed it next to her plate.

Jake cleared his throat and tugged at his collar.

Carlotta studied the expressions of the other patrons—the raised eyebrows, the hushed tones, forks paused in midair.

Jake grabbed her hands. "Come on, now. You don't mean all of that." He flashed his signature smile, albeit weakly.

Nice try, buddy.

Not even the orchestral music in the background could calm her nerves. Carlotta pulled back her hands and willed them to stop shaking. OK, so usually she didn't mean it, but this time, she would follow through, prove to her sister that she wasn't a...what was the term—co-dependent. Plenty of heroines in stories summoned the courage to do difficult things. She could do it, too. "I'm calling an attorney first thing in the morning, Jake."

She clutched her purse and stood. Adrenaline surged inside her, and heat crept up her face. What were they looking at? Returning the stare of other patrons, she took a deep breath, reached inside her purse, and tossed a few bills on the table. "This should cover the tip. I'll stay with my sister tonight. I'll pick up my things tomorrow." Amazing how easy it was to keep walking away from the table once she set her feet in motion. Carlotta exited the restaurant. Jake hadn't followed her, hadn't tried to stop her. He didn't believe her. But he would once the divorce papers arrived.

Carlotta blew out a breath. So this was it for her and Jake. She clutched her cross necklace for strength. How would she break this to her family? They weren't super spiritual, per se, but they were steeped in religious tradition. Divorce was pretty taboo. Then again, times were changing. Cousin Isabella had divorced. At least she had a child. Carlotta had a kitten. Better than nothing but not quite the same. It didn't quench her desire to be a mother.

She went outside the restaurant and choked back a sob. Why did he have such power over her? Carlotta sniffled. She'd dated other guys, but Jake was her first true love. That was long ago. Back when he cherished her. Or maybe he didn't mean it then either.

Carlotta stepped forward.

HONK. Screech.

Where had the car come from?

"Watch where you're going," the driver hollered and sped away.

Carlotta inhaled a deep breath. *Pretend you're a feisty character in a story. Just fake it. You can do this.* When the light changed, she crossed the street, sat on a bench, and dialed the number on the seat. "Hello? Yes, I'm at the corner of Main and Fifth. I need a taxi ride."

"We can send someone there in ten minutes," a raspy voice answered.

"Thank you." Carlotta hung up and dialed her sister. "Rosario, I did it."

"Did what?"

"I'm leaving Jake. I'm calling a divorce attorney tomorrow. Can I stay at your place tonight?" She swiped a tear.

"It's not like you can stay with him. I'll leave the front light on. See you in a few. I'll make some coffee. Oh, and be careful. There's been a black cat in the neighborhood recently. You don't need any more bad luck."

Carlotta shook her head. Her sister and her superstitions. "And you'll read about it in the papers, so you might as well know..." She softened her voice. "Ed Gorman is dead. I found his body earlier this week."

"What?" her sister gasped. "You don't think Pablo did it?" she whispered.

"No," her voice caught a little, "but Jake gave his

name to the police."

"He did what?"

Carlotta quelled an urge to defend him. She didn't need to do that anymore. "We'll talk more once I get there." An SUV honked at a minivan, startling her. She shifted her attention to laughter from across the street. Happy-looking couples walked together. Carlotta swiped at another tear.

She returned her phone to her purse. For once, Rosario wouldn't suggest counseling. Rosario's estranged husband, Pablo, had a drug problem. But this was completely different. Perhaps counseling worked for Rosario, but it wasn't as though Mom's addiction affected Carlotta. This thing with Jake. It was all on him. "I don't need any help," she mumbled to herself.

A cab stopped in front of her bench. Carlotta inhaled a deep breath, opened the cab door, and climbed inside. She slumped onto the seat and exhaled.

"Where to?" the cabbie asked.

Carlotta detected a southern drawl in the man's voice. "Erie Avenue, 2747."

The cabbie pulled away from the curb and headed toward the library.

Jake had said things had become mechanical. He wasn't wrong. Maybe she was making a mistake.

As the vehicle continued down the street, Carlotta muttered. "What have I done?"

"Excuse me, ma'am?"

Carlotta shook her head. "Nothing. I'm fine. Just thinking out loud." She shifted her gaze out the taxi window. A prostitute stood on a street corner. Carlotta's shoulders tightened. Where would Jake spend tonight? She huffed. Probably in the arms of that woman from work. Had she driven him away by leaving? She reached for her cell phone. What if she called him and forced him to switch jobs? Then he couldn't see what's-her-face. "Could you take me back to the restaurant?"

"Did you leave something behind?" Her gaze met the cabbie's stare in the rearview mirror.

Carlotta shifted her gaze to her purse. *Don't do this. He's the problem. The only solution is to leave him.* "Never mind. We don't need to turn around." *That's right. Keep moving.*

The taxi pulled into the parking lot of the library.

Carlotta paid her fare and opened the door. She leaned back inside and stared at the cabbie's cowboy hat. Unusual, and yet, people considered Cincinnati the northernmost southern point in the U.S. "Can you wait until I get to my car before you leave?"

"No time. Sorry."

Her stomach muscles constricted. She hurried to her vehicle, unlocked the car, and jumped into the driver's seat. Once inside, she locked the driver's side door, flipped on the interior light, and studied the backseat, almost as carefully as she checked books returned to the library for signs of damage.

All those urban legends she'd heard as a child—where did the creeps hide in cars, waiting to pop out? Carlotta looked twice more before heading out. While stopped at the light, she peered once again in the backseat. Still, no one there.

Carlotta arrived at the duplex and hugged her sister. "Oh, Rosie."

Rosario put her finger to her mouth. "Shh. Antonio is in the other room. You'll wake him. It takes forever to get that kid to sleep. If you had children, you'd understand."

Ouch.

"I'm sorry," Rosario said. "You know what I meant." She bent down and handed Carlotta a business card. "Here, you dropped this."

Carlotta studied the print, "Geoffrey Walters, Walters and Petersheim, Attorneys at Law, specializing in divorce and family law."

Her heart skipped a beat. Didn't everything happen for a reason? Jake had committed adultery. Maybe that's why they hadn't had children. Some might call it a sign from God.

Then again, she couldn't see herself with anyone else. She pictured him with his fedora, dancing with her in their living room. She rubbed her temple. *I don't know what to think.*

~*~

Letting her walk away had been hard. But she didn't mean what she said. Carlotta never did. She needed to blow off some steam. Jake rubbed the base of his neck and then patted his back pocket. Whew. At least he hadn't forgotten his wallet. Once he paid the bill, he'd look for her in the front lobby. She couldn't have gone too far.

He scanned the room for the server. Other patrons stared and then turned away. He'd brought Carlotta here so she wouldn't make a scene. So much for that. Heat crept up his cheeks.

He took one last bite of shrimp. Better savor the succulent flavor. It would probably be the last meal out for a while. His penance would include staying at home with Carlotta, watching chick flicks, and buying her flowers and candy. Jake bit his lip. As it should be.

He'd messed up big time. Hopefully, six months from now, a year, maybe…this thing would blow over. Just like the infertility problem. At some point, Carlotta had to realize it wouldn't happen according to her plan, and Jake could get his carefree wife back.

The server brought the bill, and Jake slipped his card in the billfold and handed it back. The man groaned and plodded away.

Jake's cell played a jazz tune. *Allison.* He'd let it go to voicemail and then would block her number when he got home. He wasn't her sweetie. If she needed to reach him, she could do so at work. And only there. Jake didn't need a degree in journalism to tell him that woman was bad news. *What was I thinking when I went out with her?* He grunted. *That's just it. I wasn't.*

He should have simply talked to Carlotta instead. Jake scrubbed a hand over his face. He couldn't remember a lot about what had happened. They'd gone out for drinks and talked. He must have drunk too much.

Sighing, the server returned Jake's credit card.

"May I have another card, sir? This one won't go through."

"What?" Jake ran his fingers over the creased piece of plastic. He grabbed a newer credit card and handed it to the server. "Try this one, man."

Minutes later, the server returned with the second card. "Thank you, sir."

And now to find Carlotta. A petite brunette wearing pink reclined on a bench and faced the window, back toward him. "Carlotta." The woman spun around. Jake's shoulders slumped. "Oh, sorry. I thought you were someone else." Probably in the bathroom, checking out her figure. So she'd gained a few pounds recently. That wasn't why he'd spent time with Allison. Not that Carlotta would believe him. Where was she?

He waited five more minutes before the maître d' flashed him a look that told him he should head outside. Jake stood and approached the man. "Did a brunette come through here earlier? She was wearing a pink shirt."

The man answered him without meeting his gaze, his stare transfixed on a list of reservations. "Yes, several minutes ago."

Hurrying outside, Jake glimpsed Carlotta hopping into a taxi. "Carly!"

The vehicle started up and traveled down the street.

Jake sprinted toward the parking lot. Broken glass fragments crunched under his loafers.

Where was his car? No. They couldn't have. Oh,

but they had. They'd towed his car. His muscles quivered, and his nostrils flared. Expletives took turns exiting his mouth like type hammers pounding the page. He hadn't parked his car there that long. How could he follow Carlotta?

Jake didn't have to follow her. It was play-it-safe Carlotta. She was bound to be at home, waiting for him, madder than an editor waiting on a byline, but home.

His cell rang. "Hello?"

"It's Randy."

Maybe he could ask him for a ride.

"Several ducks were found dead at Eden Park. It could be related to the dead dogs at the shelter. More proof of the triad, dude."

"Maybe someone tossed them some aged, moldy bread. Or they died of natural causes."

"That attorney, Sheryl Williams, was jogging after work and stopped to examine the dead ducks. She said a person wearing all black tried to run her down with their car and then got out on foot and tried to kidnap her, but she got away. Which means the kidnapper was—"

Jake's mouth fell open. "Still there after he killed the animals."

"Yep. Your wife is lucky. And to clarify, we don't know it's a him. The victim said a tall person in black. She didn't hear their voice. The kidnapper wore all black and a mask, so it could have been a tall chick."

"I doubt it." Jake chuckled. "Hey, you said the kidnapper wore all black? You sure it's not the ghost woman everyone's talking about—the one who supposedly roams the area near the park?"

Randy huffed. "Don't be ridiculous, dude. The ghost lady...err, Imogene, wears all black and a black hat and not a mask. And yes, it could be a woman. Plenty of chicks are tall. Allison's almost your height. Sheesh, she tore out of here earlier. Tried to follow you, I think. Speaking of which, did you two, um, well, you know—"

Jake cleared his throat. So much for the idea of getting a ride with Randy. "I've gotta go." Going out with Allison for drinks after work had been a stupid mistake. One that everyone in the office would know about. A part of him wanted to find Carlotta and move as far away from here as possible. Then again, he'd have to stick it out longer for that promotion. Maybe then they could leave.

His mind flashed back to the present problem. He needed a vehicle. Jake scrambled to the bus stop on the corner and glanced at his watch. At least fifteen more minutes until the bus arrived. And that was assuming it arrived on schedule. Jake twisted his watch repeatedly. The pink neon sign showed the adjacent convenience store was open. He approached the elderly balding clerk by the register. "Five lottery scratch-offs, please." Jake retrieved his wallet from his pocket.

"That'll be five dollars," the man said.

Jake handed the clerk the money and snatched the scratch cards from the man's fingers. He sat on a bench near the bus stop and retrieved a coin from his pocket.

Adrenaline rushed through his body. He scratched the first. Nothing. Oh, well, four more to go. He scratched the second and the third and the fourth.

An elderly woman had taken a seat on the other end of the bench. She reminded him of Granny. Grandma wouldn't have approved of the foul language he wanted to say, and he didn't figure this woman would either. He looked down at the scratch-offs in his hand. No, Granny wouldn't have approved of his gambling either, or the affair with Allison. Granny lived her life according to the Bible. Maybe there was something to that.

The elderly woman clutched her purse and raised an eyebrow.

Jake scratched the last card. Nothing. He tore up the scratch-offs and threw them in the trash.

As the bus approached, Jake stood. The woman boarded the vehicle. Jake followed. A musty odor pervaded his bench seat. A chill swept over him. Jake rubbed his arms and looked around. What if someone had been at the animal shelter, waiting and watching Carlotta when she arrived? His heart pounded at the thought.

The bus stopped a block from the bungalow he and Carlotta called home. Jake went through the front door. No sign of Carlotta. The light flashed on the landline. He dialed into voicemail. A message from Detective Hadley. The police wanted to talk to Carlotta again.

He fed the kitten, and the gray fur ball pranced behind him into the living room. Jake reclined on the couch, and the kitten snuggled next to him. "You need a name. How about Gracie?" The kitten purred its approval.

Jake shifted his gaze from the clock to the TV. Carlotta was probably taking her time. Maybe on purpose to make him suffer. She'd be home soon. His lids heavy, he gave into the temptation to rest his eyes for a while.

4

As day broke through the living room window of the Hyde Park Craftsman-style home, a realization swept over Jake. Carlotta had left him. Which meant he had to work harder to get her back. The painful truth became clear. If he'd simply spent as much time working on their marriage as he had on that promotion...or talked to a counselor about what happened, maybe he wouldn't be in this position.

Had she found out about the gambling, too? He'd had some periodic binges, but nothing too shocking. He'd borrowed some money from Granny once. Jake took darting glances at the photo of his grandmother on the fireplace mantel. His chest tightened.

His cell phone rang. Definitely Allison. He must put an end to this.

One night out with a coworker after work. A few drinks, not even that much. Several people there and then just Allison and him. What happened next was a blur. "Allison?"

"No, it's Stu! You know, the man who signs your checks." his boss said, an edge to his voice.

Jake coughed. "Sorry." At least he hadn't violated any of Stu's rules recently. That ought to count for something.

"You heard about the attempted kidnapping at the park?"

"Eden Park?"

"That's the one. Oh, and I heard about what happened at the animal shelter. Get a statement. I want a write-up as soon as possible. Can't trust any of the other nitwits with my top stories."

Jake suppressed a laugh and scribbled a reminder.

"And take the back entrance to the office. The fuzz are everywhere. A pipe bomb exploded in the mailroom."

He jerked his head back. "What? Is anyone...?"

"No one was here. Lucky for the mail guy. Bomb contained nails. They flew everywhere."

Jake flinched. Thank goodness he hadn't run into Pencil Boy and his mail cart yesterday. First the animal shelter, now pipe bombs. What was going on?

"All we need right now. Publicity." Stu huffed.

Jake popped a coffee pod into the coffeemaker, and turned on the machine. "Any idea on who—?"

"Some nut job or whackadoo who's holding a grudge. I'm taking my wife out for our anniversary. Think you can handle the cops?"

The red light on the coffee machine blinked. Jake sighed and added water to the machine. "Sure thing." Jake should be thankful Stu trusted him enough to talk to the police, considering Stu didn't trust many people. Plus, to make senior editor, he had to be in Stu's good graces—not a simple task for anyone. His boss had a mental list of possible offenses longer than the front page of the newspaper.

"Good. You know what I say…"

"Avoid the authorities like the plague?" Jake suppressed a chuckle. He glanced at the coffeemaker. Some caffeine would do him good.

"And don't forget about the jogger incident and the animal shelter. Doesn't your wife volunteer there? Talk to her." Stu hung up.

After pouring some coffee in a to-go cup, Jake sighed. *Ugh. Still need to retrieve my car from the impound.* He called for a cab.

Jake replayed Stu's words. *Your wife.* Now if only he could find her. He headed to the front door and cast a glance at the dusty Bible on the bookshelf. Grandma would've told him to pray about it. Jake huffed. Things weren't that desperate. Besides, given his adultery, who knew what might happen if he touched the pages.

~*~

After retrieving his car and handling an interview with the police at work, Jake hurried to his first assignment. He glanced around Sheryl Williams' quaint neighborhood and knocked on the door of the brick home. A slender, dark-haired woman wearing a bright blue jogging suit answered. "Hello, how may I help you?"

"I'm Jake Hartman, a journalist with the local newspaper. I called about an interview. Do you still have time to do this?" *Time. Ugh.* He needed to talk to Carlotta, preferably face to face.

Sheryl chuckled. "Sure. I almost forgot, but it's

OK. I have time. Come on in and have a seat." She motioned to an empty chair.

Jake eyed the living room. and spied a package on her coffee table. His shoulders tensed. The pipe bombs. What if someone sent one to the house, and Carlotta went over there and tried to open it? He'd call her the moment the interview ended.

Sheryl settled into a chair across from him. "Is everything OK? Can I get you something?"

"No, I'm good." He adjusted his collar. "I...just remembered something I need to do later. Why don't you tell me about what happened in the park?"

Sheryl smiled. "I was going for a jog near Eden Park as I normally do."

"So you go there regularly?"

"Yeah, so I suppose someone could have figured that out and watched me before that day. There were these dead ducks at the park. I got closer to them and felt this arm around my face. Someone had grabbed me. I fought back. The attacker wore all black and had on a black mask."

"How did you escape?"

"I screamed, and a man came running to my aid. I was very fortunate."

"Did you hear the kidnapper's voice?"

The woman shook her head. "No...but they smelled familiar. I can't describe it. Just a well-known smell."

Jake stood to shake her hand. "Thank you."

Her gaze met his and lingered. "Have we met before?" She gave him a once over.

Heat crept up his face. He averted his gaze. "I don't think so."

Sheryl's gaze narrowed. "Wait, I think I know. Did you—"

Jake's phone buzzed. He glanced at the display. "My boss. Sorry, I have to take this. Thank you. Good-bye." He slipped out of the house.

Sheryl waved and closed her door.

For more privacy, Jake got into his car. "Hello? Stu? Another pipe bomb? I'll be there as soon as I can." He hung up the phone and glanced back at Sheryl's home. She did look kind of familiar. Oh, well, maybe he could look her up in the archives another day. Given as many people as he'd interviewed— politicians, athletes, coaches, crime victims—their paths might have intersected before. Unless such knowledge could help solve the mystery of who sent pipe bombs to the newspaper, it wasn't as important.

~*~

A knock sounded on the front door. Carlotta checked the clock. Rosario should be at work unless Antonio was sick, and she had to bring him home.

Carlotta laid her cell phone on the scuffed-up coffee table. She'd received a new text from Jake.

Carly. He was the only one who called her that. Maybe she should go home. But he'd slept with another woman. How could she overlook that? Then again, maybe if she hadn't been so focused on having children lately, he wouldn't have strayed. They'd both grown apart.

She peered out the peephole. No one stood there. Carlotta unlocked the deadbolt. A bouquet of red roses lay atop the doorstep. Didn't Jake know by now that roses wouldn't fix things? This was bigger than one of his gambling binges. He'd messed up big time. This was the kind of offense that *cuesta un ojo de la cara*. She shook her head. No, not even an eye from his face would suffice. Her nostrils flared. What if he really had meant to only talk to the blonde? It wasn't like Jake to cheat.

It was also unlike Jake to knock and then run away. Carlotta crossed her arms. Good thing Lopez women were strong. Every one of them. Exactly like *Abuela* had taught them. Carlotta put on her running shoes along with a baseball cap. She locked the door and jogged as far as the corner. No sign of Jake, yet the hairs on her neck stood on edge as they did when she was little. She and Rosario would sneak pastries from Grandma's kitchen, but Grandpa would find them. Grandpa sure wasn't watching now. But then, who? Jake, maybe?

A sweaty hand wrapped itself around her mouth while a second found its way around her waist. *Ay, chihuahua!* She tried to scream, but the hand muffled her voice. Now what? She launched her hands on her attacker's and tried to pry them off. No use. *Don't give up!* Using her feet, she stomped on the attacker's shoes.

"Ouch," he screeched.

She pulled again on his hands and stomped again. Was this the same person who'd killed Ed and the dogs at the animal shelter? Perhaps part of the triad Jake had mentioned? If Ed hadn't survived, how could she? Carlotta glanced around. Where were all the neighbors when she needed them?

"We've gotta talk. Get in the car," the man with a muffled voice said.

Familiar sounding, but she had trouble placing it. Was it Xavier from the library? Or Oliver, her ex-boyfriend?

No way. If she stepped in the car, she'd be dead for sure. She attempted to wriggle free from her captor, but he maintained his grip. She jerked her head around to face her assailant, but he held onto one arm. "What do you—?"

"Please get in the car, Rosario."

Rosario? So they wanted her sister. She struggled to piece the puzzle together. What sort of criminal said please?

"I didn't kill him," the man said.

Was he referring to Ed? Why did she know that voice? Was her attacker a regular patron at the library? Maybe that creepy guy who came once a week and asked for books on chess. No, he had a noticeable speech impediment.

The man spun her around and studied her appearance. He yanked off her baseball cap. "You ain't Rosario." The assailant released his grip.

Carlotta huffed and then blew out a breath. "And you're not Jake. Pablo, just what exactly do you think you're doing?"

Her brother-in-law crossed his arms. "Where's

your reporter husband? You know the cops wanna talk to me? Your boss got killed, and now they think I did it. I promise I ain't done nothing." Pablo cradled his face in his hands.

Carlotta rubbed the back of her neck. Drug use didn't make Pablo a murderer. Plus, if she had to guess, drugs, though harmful, had temporarily helped Pablo overcome the horrors of military combat he'd experienced. Different from his drug addiction days, he sported a white, short-sleeve shirt and khakis. He had the scent of cologne, not weed. No needle marks. Normal-looking pupils, too. "Pablo, take it easy. Rosario and I don't think you had anything to do with Ed's death."

Pablo quirked a brow. "You don't?"

Sure, he could have killed Ed. He had a motive, but if he was the killer, wouldn't he have killed her just now? Nah, it had to be someone else. Carlotta rested on the front steps of the duplex. "No, and Jake won't be my husband much longer." It sounded so foreign when said aloud. Not a good sound either.

Pablo sat next to her and grabbed her arm. "You're getting separated, too?"

"Not separated. Divorced."

"Divorced?" Pablo's eyes widened. "What about your family?" Pablo gestured to the concrete statue of a saint in a neighbor's yard. "What about the church?" He gazed toward the sky. "What about God?"

"Are you judging me? What about you and my sister?"

"Look, that's different. We're separated. Rosario

just needs some time."

Carlotta chuckled. "She's had time, Pablo. Face it. She's moved on."

Pablo's shoulders slumped.

"You still love her. Have you told her?"

He shook his head. "She won't talk to me. Not that I can blame her. Thought maybe I could make her listen."

"At least someone's in love." She rested a hand on his shoulder. "You can't go about doing things like this. No more sneaking around. I found my boss dead. I can't take too many more scares. Got it?"

Pablo reached toward her. "Help me."

"I can't help my marriage, let alone yours."

"What did Jake do?"

Carlotta rolled her eyes. "You mean what did he and the blonde do?"

Pablo nodded. "Oh, that one he works with." His eyes widened. "Oh, yeah, I remember her."

She cleared her throat. "Not helping."

"Does he want to get back together?"

"I don't know. Maybe you didn't hear me. He committed adultery."

"Guys do dumb stuff all the time. If he's sorry, I say you give him a second chance."

"And what if he cheats again? Then what? Nice flowers, by the way."

"What flowers?"

She thumbed to the bouquet on the steps. "The roses. At first, I thought maybe Jake sent them. But when I saw you...oh, I assumed you sent them to

Rosario." A chill swept over her. Had Jake sent them? If not, then who? No one else knew she was staying there. Maybe they were for Rosario, from someone other than Pablo. Or perhaps the florist got mixed up, and the flowers were for the duplex residents next door. She reviewed a note attached to the bouquet.

Roses are red,

Violets are blue,

Librarians are sweet,

I see you.

Carlotta crumpled the note. Definitely wasn't for Rosario. Someone was targeting her. Jake wouldn't be so creepy. Who would send them?

~*~

Jake entered the worn brick neighborhood coffee shop that evening and savored the pungent aroma as his shoes clacked across the original wood floor. Detective Kelsey Krouse sat at a table in the corner. Maybe he could press her for more information about what happened at the animal shelter.

He waved to her and then approached the front counter of the establishment. For a moment, he took in all the industrial-looking renovations the new owner had made to the building before the coffee shop opened a month earlier. "Double espresso. Black, please."

When the barista finished his order, she handed the coffee to him. He joined Kelsey at her table.

Jake retrieved his cell phone and set it on the table.

Kelsey wrapped her hands around her own cup.

Leaning closer, Jake inhaled the warm fragrance from his coffee.

Kelsey had the local newspaper open to page five.

He swallowed. "The missing woman story?"

"Yeah. Tonya Miller. A college student. Only twenty." She folded the paper shut.

Maybe it was her smile, easygoing nature, or pleasant southern drawl, but something about Krouse made her easy to talk to. Mental face palm. *Don't go down that road again.* That's how it had started with Allison. Just chatting with a coworker. A few drinks. And then waking up in her bed the next morning. His chin dipped to his chest, and his shoulders slumped. "I have a few questions about what happened at the animal shelter."

"Sorry, Jake."

He flashed a smile. *C'mon, Kelsey. Help me out here.* "Off the record. Between friends? I know you can't give details, but maybe some hints here or there."

"No can do. Sorry."

"OK. I understand." He clenched his coffee cup tighter. He'd have to find his information elsewhere.

"I heard about the pipe bombs at your office. I'm glad you're OK." Krouse sipped her coffee.

"We get threats from weirdoes occasionally. Guess I'm sort of on high alert for now."

Krouse nodded and blinked. "How's your wife doing? Still shook up?"

He avoided Krouse's gaze. "Uh, yeah, I guess you could say that. We're not exactly speaking much right now. I'm pretty sure she's moved in with her sister. It's complicated."

"I'm sorry to hear that. Would it be OK if I prayed for you?" She leaned closer and invaded his personal space.

Jake scanned the room to see if anyone else was watching. "Uh, sure."

"God…"

He shut his eyes. His insides churned. Public prayer had never been his style. Plus, what if Carlotta saw them? Not as though she'd believe they were only talking and praying.

"Please be with Jake and his wife. You know the situation, and I ask for healing of their relationship and for peace, Your peace, for both of them. Draw them closer to You. Amen."

"Uh, Amen."

Something was different about Kelsey. Krouse was friendly but not in the same way as Allison. She behaved professionally, always met him in a public place, and never hit on him. Kelsey genuinely cared for people. Religious, but the real deal. Very admirable.

5

Carlotta inhaled the warm steam from the shower, massaged her shoulder with soap, and released a pent-up breath.

Mom drank to overcome her past. Dad used relationships and work to escape his pain. She got over Mom and Dad, and she'd get over Jake, too.

No, no she wouldn't.

Carlotta clenched the soap and scrubbed her other shoulder. Warm water cascaded as she inhaled and exhaled the steam. Did she really want to wash him out of her life? If only there was another way.

She toweled the water from her body, and shrugged on the white t-shirt and jeans borrowed from her sister. She tugged at the neckline—more revealing than fit her taste. Her sister always dressed younger than her age. Rosario could get away with being capricious. Not her, not the oldest.

The sun shone in through the semi-opaque window. No storms. Just bright and sunny. Maybe like her new life. With her in control. Not Dad. Not Mom. Not Jake. But what about God? Where did He fit in? Too early to think about.

Her mind flashed to the roses and the note she'd found by Rosario's front door. She'd dispose of them later. No need to mention them to her sister.

A knock sounded on the bathroom door.

"Are you OK?" Rosario called from the other side.

Carlotta flung open the door and stepped outside the mint green bathroom. "Thanks for the clothes, Rosario."

A spider scurried across the weathered hardwood floor. Carlotta gasped and jumped.

Rosario laughed and squished it with her white tennis shoe. "I see you still can't kill bugs."

"I have the day off, and I need to get some things from the house. Maybe check for mail. Do you want to come with me?"

"Sorry, I have to work today. I was supposed to have the day off, but another cashier called in sick." Rosario pinned a nametag onto her white shirt and cracked her neck. "Why are you picking up your stuff? Shouldn't Jake be the one to move out?"

"I need a clean slate. I was hoping maybe…" Carlotta cleared her throat. "I could stay and help watch Antonio for you, so you could go out in the evenings."

"Hm." Rosario nodded. "Do you think you could start by dropping Antonio off at daycare on your way to pick up your things?"

"Sure. How's Pablo doing? You getting back together soon? Antonio needs his father."

Rosario crossed her arms. "What do you know about kids?"

Carlotta's mouth fell open.

"I'm sorry. That wasn't right. It's just that it's not

your business, and I don't want to talk about it with Antonio around." Rosario strode toward the door and grabbed her purse from atop an antique oak coffee table.

Carlotta shifted her gaze to the living room. No Antonio in sight. "You have to leave right now?"

Rosario nodded. "Gotta be there on time. I'm not on good terms with one of the higher ups at work. Have to make a good impression in case an assistant management position opens up." She pointed to the cabinets. "Cereal is in the cupboard. Milk's in the fridge. Make sure Antonio eats and gets out of his pajamas before you take him to daycare. I already installed the car seat in your car."

"Thanks." She clamped her mouth shut. Rosario didn't need to do that. She was barren, not clueless. Carlotta waved to her sister. How long would she stay with Rosario? Could she afford her own place? The only other option was to move in with Mom, and that wasn't happening.

Once breakfast was over, Carlotta strapped Antonio in the car seat. A little difficult but not too bad. Her nephew was adorable. Too bad she and Jake hadn't had any children. But maybe it was better this way. Still, she couldn't help but think he would have made a good father. He'd certainly impressed her with how he'd interacted with the kids in their neighborhood, even volunteering as a Big Brother for one of them after their father died.

On the drive to daycare, Carlotta released a pent-up breath and sang two nursery rhymes. Her cell rang, and she pulled into the parking lot of a nearby store before answering it. "Hello?"

"Hi, Carlotta. This is Wendy from Fresh Start Homeless Shelter. Last month, you helped us out. We need some volunteers again. I realize this is short notice, but can you help us out tonight?"

"Um, sure." Carlotta's shoulders tensed a little as she worked her way through her mental checklist. Drop Antonio off. Go pick up her things and head to work. Then volunteer tonight. No problem. What kind of person would she be if she turned them down?

With Antonio safely at daycare, Carlotta drove to her house. A wilted patch of red and pink tulips and yellow and white daffodils lined the sidewalk. Her own garden—as dilapidated as the state of her marriage.

Carlotta might not be able to save her marriage, but perhaps she should dig up her perennials and take them with her.

Jake's car wasn't in the driveway.

Carlotta found an empty box in the hall closet. Inside, she placed her houseplants—Mary, Jane, Lydia, Kitty, and Elizabeth. Next, she gathered up her toiletries. Needles and pills caught her eye. No need to take fertility medication anymore. Relief flooded her. She stuffed her daily wardrobe into three leather suitcases and carried the first two out to the car, followed by another trip for the box of plants.

She gazed at the photo of Jake and her on the mantel. Carlotta squeezed her eyes shut. Could she forgive Jake? Yes, he'd done something wrong, but they'd had good times, too.

The gray kitten Jake had found skittered into view. It meowed and followed her around. So cute, but she couldn't take it with her. Rosario was allergic to cats. Maybe Jake could find it another home.

The doorbell rang. Better not be Jake. She opened the door, suitcase in hand.

A blonde on the other side of the doorstep crossed her arms. A tattoo of bright red lips peeked out from her blouse, while a second, a red and black pitchfork, snaked around her ankle and up part of her calf. "Is Jake here?"

Gripping the doorframe tighter, Carlotta fought the urge to use words no lady should utter. But considering the company wasn't exactly polite… "May I help you?" she asked through gritted teeth.

"I need to talk to him…about an assignment." Blondie smiled.

Carlotta pressed her lips together. *Assignments.* Is that what they were calling it these days? "I don't know where he is. But here, you can give him this." Carlotta retrieved the mail by the door and stole one quick glance at the box before shoving it toward the woman. "Just look at the tape all over this. Addressed to Jake Heartman." She chuckled. *Didn't even spell their last name correctly. Theirs.* But for how much longer?

Blondie examined the package.

After she lugged her suitcase outside, Carlotta locked the door behind her and moved around Blondie. To think she might have crawled back to Jake. Rosario was right about the need for counseling. She'd find love again, but not until she could trust herself not to make the same mistakes.

What if counseling could help her and Jake? Was it too late at this point? She'd pushed him into infertility treatments. Maybe that's what caused the change in his behavior.

Once she pulled into Rosario's driveway, Carlotta checked her cell. One missed call and a message. She dialed voicemail and entered her passcode. "Hello, this is Detective Hadley with the Cincinnati Police Department. I have a few additional questions for you regarding the incident at the animal shelter. If you could call me at your earliest convenience, I'd appreciate it." A chill swept over her. Were more dogs killed? What if something happened again? Who would she contact? Rosario? Jake? He'd protected her before. Would he still want to, or would he be busy with the blonde woman?

While at work, another librarian raved about the benefits of having a handgun. Perhaps it wouldn't be a bad idea. Only as a precaution. Besides, odds were if she purchased it, she'd never need it. How often did one really use a weapon?

~*~

Jake slammed his car door, grabbed his coffee and *goetta* from the corner shop, and took a minute to savor the aroma of both before sauntering up his driveway.

Allison leaned against the front of his house in a revealing outfit.

Jake forced his gaze to meet hers. What was she doing here?

"I'm happy to see you, too." Allison smirked. "Here, this came in the mail for you."

Jake examined the poor packaging and misspelling. "Give me that."

"What if I don't?" Allison quirked a brow.

"There were pipe bombs at the office. That package is suspicious. Give it to me. I don't think we should open it." Jake snatched the package, gently set it on the grass on the other side of the lawn but away from the sidewalk, and then hurried back to the front of his house. He eyed the package again, pointed to it, and gazed at Allison. "This is my home address. Why were you going through my mail?"

"I wasn't. Carlita gave it to me. Must have come in the mail yesterday."

He sighed. "Carlotta."

"Don't worry, darling." She twirled an errant strand of hair. "The wife isn't here. She left a little while ago."

"She came here?" He bit back a curse. "When?"

Allison shrugged. "I don't know, hon. Around seven thirty. She carried a suitcase." She put a hand on his shoulder and leaned closer. Hot, lemony-scented breath blew in his direction. Even lemons couldn't cover the stench of alcohol on her breath. "I asked her where you were." Allison had listened to his problems. Her only other positive qualities were skin deep.

He backed away. "Wait, you talked to her?" Carlotta would assume the worst. And why shouldn't she? Ugh. "We need to talk. I made a mistake."

She knitted her brows. "What are you saying, sweetie?"

"I should never have gone out for drinks with you. There can't be anything between us. I love Carlotta."

Laughing, Allison leaned closer and blew hot breath on his neck. "Randy is right. You do have a sense of humor."

He leaned away. "I'm serious."

She studied his face. "You are serious." A scowl replaced her grin. She crossed her arms. Her voice softened, and her expression changed. "We could just talk."

Jake blocked her. "Uh-uh." He just wanted a shoulder to lean on, someone to confide in… He'd been so desperate he'd ignored clear warning signs. Bright red ones he could no longer brush aside.

Allison shook her head. A devilish smile spread across her face. "You'll be sorry, hon," she spoke in a singsong voice with much emphasis on the last phrase. She slinked back to her car and climbed inside.

Jake stomped away. Be sorry? He was already there.

The SUV's wheels screeched as Allison sped away.

He did his best to block her from his mind and focus on more important matters. Jake marched into the bathroom. No perfume, no makeup. All gone. If Carlotta picked up her things, she must be staying somewhere else. And as he'd surmised, there was only one place she'd go. Rosario's. He dialed her cell. "Is Carlotta with you?"

"No. Is this Jake? Carlotta went to work. Tomorrow, she's meeting with an attorney. You know, it's real this time. She's leaving you."

A dial tone buzzed in his ears. He punched a pillow and then hurled it across the room. *Carlotta is leaving. Just like you probably told her to.* Exactly why he didn't care for Rosario at times. She could be controlling.

If he wanted to win Carlotta back, he needed to ease up on his control, treat her differently. A little voice nagged him. Tell her why he wanted to adopt? As though that would matter.

He bit his lip. Carlotta's fertility treatments cost a lot of money. And so did adoption. His mind flashed to the lottery tickets he'd purchased recently. The state lottery total had soared to fifty million.

Jake's cell rang. Where'd he put his phone? He patted his pockets until he located it. "Hello?"

"Hey, this is Bob Hathaway, from the men's Bible study group at Cincinnati Evangelical Free Church. There's a retreat coming up in a month, and I wanted to invite you. It'd be the second weekend in July at a camp in rural Indiana, two hours away from here. Are you interested? Even has a zip line."

"I'll think about it, man, and I'll give you an answer shortly." A zip line sounded like fun. But a Bible study. Were adulterers welcome?

"Sounds good. Hope to see you soon."

"Thanks. Maybe I can attend the group next week. Bye." He clutched his cell phone in his hand.

A retreat? With church people. Maybe some

meditation would do him some good.

He stumbled into a chair and sank into it. The kitten joined him. He petted Gracie's fluffy fur. Somewhat calming, given the circumstances.

To save his marriage, he could switch jobs, and the social connections from church could prove useful. He swallowed hard. All that work to try to make it to Senior Editor. But, as Granny would have said, he made his own mess, and now he needed to clean it up. Good old Granny. She would have liked Carlotta. Isn't that what attracted him to her in the first place? Carlotta was so giving, like poor old Granny. So kind, and yet, Grandpa had cheated on her. Like grandfather, like grandson. Jake pinched the bridge of his nose and closed his eyes. Was there any hope for him and his marriage?

6

Carlotta headed over to re-shelve books in the nonfiction section. What a long work day. She sighed. Sometimes, when Jake was in the area working on a story, he'd stop by and have lunch with her. But now she'd moved out. What if he really was sorry? Could she give him another chance? Rosario would probably accuse her of being weak. A blonde woman walked by. Her mind flashed to the night he'd broken the news of the affair to her. How could he have done that? They'd grown more distant lately with all the infertility treatments, but still. Carlotta balled her fists at her sides. *He should have talked to me.*

Plus, she'd received that strange note with the flowers. Jake could have sent them.

She picked up a book and studied the library call number on the book binding. Shifting her gaze back to a shelf, Carlotta attempted to find the correct position for the book.

A man behind her said, "Hi, Carlotta."

"Ah." Carlotta dropped the book. She turned. "Sorry. You frightened me. I didn't expect anyone to be there." Her gaze narrowed on Xavier. The guy with a crush on her. The one who checked out movies about killers.

"Hey, Carlotta, can you help me find some cookbooks?"

"Sure." Patrons didn't normally call her by her first name.

She led Xavier to the correct shelf.

"Did your husband watch the movie about the Zodiac killer? He writes about crime, right?"

"Uh, no." She hung her head. "My husband and I are getting a divorce." The words came out of her mouth on autopilot before she could reel them back in. Why had she shared that?

"I'm sorry to hear that. I'm going camping with the guys again." He pulled some pictures up on his phone. Some guys in tents. Then several of a skinned deer. "See, I have to prepare the meals." He scrolled through more deer and camping photos.

She averted her gaze. The deer reminded her of the dead animals at the shelter. Maybe Xavier wasn't involved with what happened that night, but he was a bit odd.

"You know, Carlotta, we should go out to lunch together sometime."

Carlotta cleared her throat. "Um. Right now?"

Xavier became more animated. "Yes, today. I know this place that just opened up around the corner. Has the best Mexican food."

"I, uh." *Think of an excuse fast.*

A soft voice came from behind her. "Miss, can you help me?"

Turning, she called back to Xavier, "Excuse me. I need to help this person."

As she walked away to help an elderly man, she relaxed her muscles. Maybe now Xavier would leave her alone. Then, later today, she could talk to her boss about what to do about Xavier.

The elderly man showed her a note with a book call number he'd scrawled on paper. "Where is this? It's a book on genealogy. I'm researching my family tree."

"OK, that will be," she pointed to several shelves over, "in that row." She led the man to the correct spot and helped him locate the book.

As she ambled away from the man, she searched left and right. And even behind. But Xavier was gone. Whew.

Grabbing an empty library cart, she took the elevator downstairs. Just need to grab some books to take upstairs. Carlotta scanned her list of holds and soon loaded up her cart. Pretty quiet work. Not too many people on the lower level.

She pushed her cart into the elevator and selected the button to go upstairs. Maybe Jake wouldn't stop by today, but she could still have a nice lunch. Maybe a quiet one where she could read a book.

The elevator doors started to close, but a hand wedged its way through. Xavier stepped inside. Had he been hiding downstairs, waiting for her?

Carlotta bit back a scream.

Xavier moved next to the elevator buttons. Today, he carried a different backpack than last time. A red and yellow circular logo patch with the letters APCC inside adorned the side. APCC? Jake had suspected they might have been responsible for the animal shelter break-in.

Carlotta's heart raced. *Have to get out of here. I'll just dart out of here when the doors open.*

Xavier grinned. Maybe a bit too much. "There you are. We can go to lunch now." He stepped closer to her.

Her throat became dry. "I, uh."

The elevator doors started to open. Xavier slapped the close doors button.

"What are you doing?" Her voice rose in pitch. "Let me out!"

"Don't be in such a hurry, Carlotta..."

Think quick. Using all her might, Carlotta pushed the cart into Xavier. She leaned toward the buttons, hitting the doors open button. "Help," she yelled.

The doors started to open. A man outside the elevator boomed. "Hey, what's going on?"

Carlotta stepped outside the elevator.

"Carly, what's the matter? Are you OK?" Jake's concerned look took in Xavier, and his face hardened.

Her eyes widened. "What are you doing here?"

"I came by as I normally do. I asked Becca where you were. She said you went downstairs, so I headed for the elevator."

Xavier scrambled out of the elevator and darted out of the library.

She shot a glance at Jake and pleaded. "He's getting away."

Jake sprinted after the man and shouted, "Get back here! Stop!" He ran out of the library but returned minutes later. He leaned over and huffed. "Was that the patron with the crush on you?"

Gripping the cart, she nodded. "Yes."

Jake put an arm around her and invaded her personal space. "Are you OK, baby?" His husky voice was swoon-worthy.

He wanted to go back to normal. But how could she trust him now? If he had cheated once, wouldn't he just cheat again? She stepped back from him. "Yes, Jake. Thank you. I'll call the police. I can handle it from here. But thank you." She was mad at him, but he had been there for her when she needed him. She could at least be civil.

Jake lowered his voice. "Are you sure you don't want me to stay with you?"

She averted her gaze and focused on the books on the cart. "Xavier had an APCC patch on his backpack. It was probably him at the animal shelter. I'll tell the police. They can catch him, and then you don't have to worry about me anymore."

Moving closer, he stared at her. "Carlotta. I will always—" His phone rang, and he groaned. "It's Stu."

She pushed her cart along. "You better go then. Thanks again." Carlotta fought the urge to stay and listen to him. If she remained longer, she just might forgive him. Safer to keep her distance for now, especially if he'd sent the note and flowers. Then again, it could have been Xavier. She rubbed her temple. Parking her cart, she picked up a book. A romance involving a cowboy. At least she could get her mind off real life for a few minutes.

~*~

As the doorbell uttered a sickly tune, Carlotta flung the door open. Her eyes widened. "Pablo?" What did she expect? That Jake would come riding over to her sister's house on a white horse and swoop her off her feet? If only.

"I'm here to talk to Rosario."

Kudos to Pablo for trying to fix his marriage. Could she and Jake do the same? Carlotta closed the door and spun around to face Pablo. "She's getting Antonio ready for bed."

Her brother-in-law followed Carlotta into the living room.

Carlotta settled into a lumpy chair across from Pablo on the stained sofa. She covered a spot with her hand. If she stayed for a while, maybe she could help Rosario with rent or help her upgrade to some newer furnishings.

Pablo cleared his throat.

Carlotta glanced at a photo of her nephew and back at Pablo. "Antonio's getting so big, you know."

"I bet. I'd love to see him." Pablo swiped a tear. "I miss him so much. Both of them, really."

Rosario roamed around the corner and cleared her throat.

"Oh, excuse me." Carlotta stood and meandered toward the kitchen. She closed the louvered doors, but stayed close by. She pressed her ear against the wooden panels.

"Thank you for meeting me, Rosario."

"We're just talking, Pablo. Don't get any ideas."

Carlotta shook her head. *Give him a chance, Rosario.* What about Jake? Should she give him another chance? Nope, not the same. At least Pablo seemed as though he might have changed.

"I've been going to church, Rosie," Pablo said, "I learned about Jesus. Got born again."

"So? We went to church before." Rosario's voice had an edge to it.

"Yeah, sometimes we did. On holidays. This is different."

"So now you're religious. That's what this is about?"

"I gave up drugs, found God. He's changed me. I used to need the drugs to cope. Now I have Jesus."

Carlotta didn't have to be in the same room to picture her sister rolling her eyes at Pablo.

"What do you want from me?" Rosario asked. "Need me to sign divorce papers? You must want something."

"I do. I want you, Rosario, and Antonio. I want you both back in my life."

"I don't know. Things were rough after you went to jail. Your son kept asking about you. And me, I had to raise a child alone. Had to find a job with flexible hours, while married to a known criminal, which didn't help my chances any. What if you go back to drugs, Pablo? Then what? Antonio and I have to start over again? How fair is that to us?"

"It wouldn't be fair. It wasn't fair the first time. I was wrong, and I'm sorry. I wanna make it up to you."

Carlotta peeked through the door slats.

Rosario crossed her arms.

Pablo touched her arm.

Rosario turned away. "I'll think about it."

Carlotta moved to get a better view through the slats. "Here." Pablo handed Rosario an envelope.

Rosario's mouth fell open. "What's this?"

"Money for Antonio and you."

"I already receive child support."

"I know. But I want you to have this. Even if you don't want to see me again, I want you to have this. Take it."

Rosario stared at the envelope. Carlotta fought back the urge to scream at her sister. *Take the money.*

After taking a step back, Rosario dangled the envelope in the air far away from her body, as if it contained poison. "Is this drug money?"

"It's a check." Pablo's shoulders dropped. "And no, it's not drug money. May I see Antonio? I haven't seen him in so long."

"I'm not sure that's a good idea. He's sort of forgotten about you. Maybe that's not a bad thing. I think maybe you better go. We can talk again later."

"OK. I'll respect that. But please think about it. I wanna see my son. Our son."

Rosario led him to the front door.

"Bye, Rosario."

"Bye, Pablo." Rosario shut the door.

Carlotta backed away.

Her sister burst through the doors. "How much did you hear?"

"Enough to know most stories don't end this way, Rosario. Pablo messed up. I get it. But he wants to make things right again. I think he's changed."

Rosario pinched her lips together. "That's the problem.... so have I."

~*~

Carlotta stood outside the brownstone building next to the animal shelter and gazed at her watch. At least her boss, Becca, had allowed her to take a longer lunch break than usual.

She went into the waiting room of Walters and Petersheim Law offices. Light yellow paint covered the walls. Conservative patterned material adorned the waiting area guest chairs next to oak coffee tables.

After two deep breaths, she approached the receptionist. "I'm here to see..." Carlotta glanced at the business card. "Mr. Walters." Jake hadn't threatened divorce. Did he still want to get back together? Maybe she should have spoken to him one more time. Maybe there was a chance of reconciliation. Could it be possible?

The young blonde receptionist smiled, revealing braces. "I'll let him know you are here."

Carlotta sat down, scanned the literature stacked on the coffee table, and settled on the newspaper. A story about pipe bombs at the paper—the building where Jake worked. No one was hurt. Carlotta set it back on the table. She checked her messages. A reminder to call Detective Hadley popped up.

She'd call him after her appointment. Mr. Walters would take her case and handle the paperwork. She wasn't ready to move on until she figured out what attracted her to men who cheated. Surely, the library had some psychology books in the self-help section. Not that she didn't want to find a knight in shining armor. Carlotta huffed. Her story was proving to be more like a tragedy than a romance with a happily ever after. And to think, Jake had once been her knight, her prince. When they were in college and he'd written for the newspaper, she couldn't wait to read his articles.

"Mr. Walters would like to apologize. He'll be with you in a few minutes."

She could still back out. Oh, but Rosario would peg her as a *cobarde* for sure. After years of getting teased by her younger sister because of her nervousness… Nope. She clenched her fists. She would not act cowardly.

The receptionist stood and opened the door to Geoffrey Walters' monochromatic gray office. "He's ready to meet with you now, Mrs. Hartman."

Even her last name sounded awkward. Would she switch back to being Carlotta Lopez? Carlotta rubbed warmth into her arms as she entered the overly air-conditioned room. For years, her identity had been wrapped up in being Mrs. Hartman, the reporter's wife. Her lips turned upward and down again.

Mr. Walters stood and quirked a brow. "How interesting. It is good to see you again, though I wish it were under better circumstances." He shook her hand a little longer than customary, and with a warm touch at that, smoothed his suit, and motioned for Carlotta to sit in a chair.

She clutched her purse. "I have confidence that our meeting today will lead to better circumstances." An insect chirped on the floor. She gasped. Dumb anxiety, always rearing its head at the wrong moment.

"Do not be frightened. It is only a hemipteran. A cicada. Must have come in because of the construction next door."

Interesting. A man who avoided contractions. He was younger than her—maybe that was how the young people spoke these days.

A drilling noise rumbled.

Mr. Walters clutched his ear. "I cannot wait until they stop remodeling this office." He looked up from his yellow legal pad, pen in hand.

"I'm considering getting a divorce from my husband."

"I see." Mr. Walters opened a drawer and removed papers.

"We don't have any children. Just a house and two cars. And a kitten, but I can't keep it anyway."

He handed her some papers. "This is the retainer agreement paperwork. It discusses fees, billing information, and who will be working on your case. Because this is a small firm, I will work with you directly. You will need to review these and sign at the bottom of the last page." He gave her several more. "These are client information forms. I need to know more about you and your spouse, including information on your finances. You can fill these out and bring them with you next time. Let us schedule our next meeting, shall we?"

"I need to look at my work schedule for the next month."

"That is fine. You can make an appointment with my secretary."

Carlotta rubbed the finger where her engagement and wedding rings used to be. Her mind flashed to when Jake had gotten down on one knee and popped the question. They'd strolled through the Magnolia Garden at Eden Park and then onto the gazebo, where he'd asked her to marry him, for better or worse. Too bad it was the latter. It hadn't all been bad. There'd been many good years. But then…. What had changed between them? Infertility. Infidelity. Creepy bouquets. Yep, that would do it.

Mr. Walters scribbled on a sheet of paper from his legal pad.

Carlotta studied his appearance—as neat as his office. As if everything in his life was in order. A person who liked to take good care of things.

Mr. Walters leaned closer and pointed to the page. "Here is my number. I would love to chat and have coffee sometime. You know, as friends. I am guessing you could use one right now. I think it is so noble how you volunteer at the rescue shelter. I am a dog lover myself."

Now why didn't Jake ever see it that way? He always thought it was silly that she spent her time volunteering or he complained it was too dangerous for her to be out at night alone. Jake wanted to move to the top. Weren't her goals—having children and volunteering—as important as his? Maybe that had been the underlying problem.

"What's your favorite breed, or are you a mutt lover?" she asked.

Mr. Walters resumed his seat, a far-off look in his eye. "My Sheltie died a year ago. I am not ready for a new dog. Not yet."

"Oh, I'm so sorry, but I understand. My dog died several years ago. I wasn't ready for a long time. I mentioned getting a dog recently, but Jake won't allow it."

"Well, after your divorce, you can have your dog." He grinned.

"I suppose so." She'd gain a dog but lose Jake. She'd rather have her husband.

Carlotta bit her lip. Would she find someone else? What would happen if another man found out she couldn't have kids? Would he feel the same way about fertility treatments as Jake, or would he push adoption? She'd have to let him know how she valued having a large family. Historically, fewer Hispanic children were available for adoption. Jake thought it was vain to want kids that looked like her, but wasn't that one reason people gave birth to biological children?

Mr. Walters cleared his throat. "You can decide where we go for coffee."

It couldn't hurt anything. Only coffee. Two people conversing over warm beverages. Besides, with Rosario's idiosyncrasies, Carlotta might need a friend to help her escape her sister's home from time to time. There was something to be said for a friend who let her call the shots now and then.

She studied the phone number on the paper and then cast a glance at Mr. Walters. "I'll let you know where and when to meet. But just as friends. I'll pay for my own coffee. We'll drive separately."

"Of course. Just as friends. I look forward to your call."

Carlotta trekked to her car. A rose lay on the windshield with a note.

Thinking about you today,

As I hum a lovely tune.

Our special day will come.

It will happen soon.

Carlotta looked around. No sign of Jake. A man jogged about half a block away down the other side of the street. A family walked into the animal shelter next door. She reread the note. Her chin trembled. "Soon…? What will happen?"

Had Xavier sent this? As far as she knew, the police hadn't found him yet.

~*~

At the end of work, Carlotta drove to Rosario's duplex. She went into the kitchen, made some coffee, and continued into the living room. She couldn't wait any longer to return the detective's call. "Hello, Detective Hadley? This is Carlotta Hartman."

"Hello, ma'am," the detective answered. "I hope

you're doing well. I only have a few questions. I won't take up too much of your time. You said you volunteer at the animal shelter. Do you have another job?"

"I work at the library." Carlotta sipped her coffee. Her new historic fiction novel was on the coffee table. Maybe now she'd get to find out how the hero rescued the girl. Assuming this call ended soon. "Is there anyone who would have reason to want to hurt you? A coworker?"

Reaching forward, she snatched her book. "There is this guy at the library. I only know his name from his library card. For years, he's chatted with me a little longer than the regular patrons. Nothing creepy. Usually looks up poetry or books about the military. Right before all this, I didn't see him for about a week. He disappeared."

"His name?"

She studied the front cover of the book. "Xavier Paxton. He finally showed up at the library again. Checked out *Catcher in the Rye*." Though a well-known classic, she'd never read it.

The detective cleared his throat.

Carlotta shifted in her seat. "What is it?"

The detective sighed. "Some say there's a link between killers and their obsession with it. Doesn't mean he's guilty of anything."

Maybe she'd have to read it to see what all the fuss was about. "Also, he checked out a copy of the movie, *Zodiac*. About the serial killer. Then he asked me to show him the true crime section of the library, but…"

"But what?" the detective asked.

"I told him my husband would like the movie because he's a news journalist. Xavier seemed embarrassed. Said he didn't know I was married. Suddenly he wasn't interested in finding more books. He wanted to leave. Said he had to meet a friend for dinner."

"Has he expressed any romantic feelings for you before?"

Hair lifted on the back of Carlotta's neck. She gazed out the living room window. Was someone watching her? "One of my coworkers seems to think so. I've never tried to encourage him in that way."

"No, ma'am. I understand. I'm not trying to imply you did. Did he give any reason for his absence?"

"He said he had gone on a camping trip with some buddies." She gulped her coffee and bounced her leg. "He showed me pictures…of their campsite and the deer he'd…cut up. And a couple days later, he sort of…trapped me in the elevator when I went downstairs to get some books that were on hold. I…shoved the cart at him as the elevator stopped, and I screamed and he ran out. I've not seen him since." The detective didn't need to know about Jake being there. It wasn't relevant.

The detective was silent for a few minutes, probably writing. Finally, he spoke again. "Anyone else? An old boyfriend, maybe."

Her leg went still. "Oliver Robertson. I was dating him right before I met my husband. He lives in Dayton. It upset him when we broke up, but this would be very out of character for him."

"One more thing. We've had another incident in which animals have been killed, though at this time, we can't prove they're related."

Another incident? Carlotta's body froze. Jake would probably know all about it. She gulped her coffee and paced the floor in agitation. Her nerves were jumping. Was someone watching her?

"I can't give any specifics, but I hoped you could think of more details from the break-in at the animal shelter, anything else you might have recalled from that night."

She bit her bottom lip. "Well, no." She backed into the corner. The person who killed Ed was still out there somewhere.

"Anything out of the ordinary? Something different or odd? Someone new in the area?"

She paced the room, casting furtive glances out the window. "No, but... Wait, you could ask Mr. Walters. He works next door and stopped by to check in on me before the police arrived. He said he heard me scream...I guess I screamed when I found...the bodies. The dogs. Ed..." Bile rose in her throat. "He's an attorney."

"Thank you, ma'am. And if you think of anything else, please call."

She hung up and removed Mr. Walters's card from her purse.

Now was as good a time as any to let him know when and where she wanted to meet for coffee. With the animal shelter investigation in progress, they'd have something to discuss. And it'd be comforting to hear his voice. Her fingers trembled as she dialed. "Hello, Mr. Walters? This is Carlotta Hartman."

"Carlotta, please call me Geoffrey. Do you still want to go out for coffee? There is this café on Red Bank Road, near the post office."

"I know the one." So did Jake. Hopefully, he wouldn't be in the area. He might get the wrong idea about her new friend. Yes, he'd done what he'd done. It didn't mean she wanted to cause him pain, too.

"I can meet you there next Monday at noon, assuming that works for you."

"That'd be great."

"Perfect. I will clear my calendar." He paused. "Can we make that the following Monday after that? I realized I have a conflicting commitment at that time."

"Sure."

"By the way, I spoke with the police. They're looking for more information regarding Ed's death and the dog slayings at the shelter. I told them you were next door. I don't know if you saw anything, but in case you did…"

A drilling noise hummed in the background. "Carlotta, I apologize, but I must prepare for going up against opposing counsel. However, I look forward to having coffee with you."

"Me, too." She hung up and shifted her position. Perhaps she should have told him about the note from Jake. Maybe later. After all, she'd just met Geoffrey Walters. She'd forgotten to mention it to the detective, too. If she got another one, then she might say something. If Jake had sent them, she didn't want to get him in trouble. He'd behaved different lately. Maybe the pressure from the infertility treatments had finally gotten to him. Extreme stress could make people do strange things. Plus, Xavier hadn't been found yet, so he was still a suspect in Carlotta's mind.

She grabbed her hamper, and trotted to the laundry room. Her phone rang. "Geoffrey?"

"Huh? It's Jake. Who's Geoffrey?"

Carlotta set her hamper on the floor. "Jake? I didn't expect to hear from you."

"Stu wants me to interview you about the break-in at the animal shelter. Purely business."

All business. Typical Jake. Carlotta opened the lid to the washer.

"You name the time and the place," Jake continued. "We can even do it over the phone if you'd rather not see me right now."

"I'll call you about coming over later. Purely business." She stuffed clothes in the washer.

"Purely business. And Carlotta…"

"What?"

His voice grew soft. "I'm sorry."

She added detergent to the washer load. The bottle spilled, pouring liquid all over the floor. Sighing, she cleaned it up. "Good-bye, Jake." Next time, she needed to confront him about the notes.

Carlotta flopped onto her bed. Sobs racked her body, and her vision blurred. The world grew silent and still, and coldness overtook her extremities. She burrowed under the comforter and fidgeted with her cross necklace. Should she pray to God for comfort?

7

A flushing sound following by a retching noise woke Carlotta.

Her sister hovered over the trashcan in the bathroom. The putrid smell of bile pierced the air.

"Rosario? Are you OK?"

Her sister shook her head. She motioned for Carlotta to go away.

The third time this month. Could someone get the stomach flu that often? And why was she the only one affected? Maybe she had a weaker stomach than everyone else. Could she be pregnant? Pablo hadn't moved back in with Rosario for any length of time since they first separated.

Rosario finally stumbled out and laid on the couch. "I'm fine. I think it's over now. It's been a long day. I started out in the deli department but ended up in the bakery. Two employees were no shows."

"Is anyone sick at work?"

Rosario shrugged. "I don't know."

"I think you should see a doctor. Maybe they can give you something."

"I probably need to throw some salt over my shoulder or find my four-leaf clover." Rosario rubbed her stomach. "Besides, doctors cost money, Carlotta."

"Maybe use the money from Pablo."

"That's for Antonio."

"Yes, and he needs his momma to be well. Or let me pay for the visit."

"Sometimes you are so stubborn. I'll make an appointment." Rosario rolled on her other side, facing away from her. "Now let me get some rest."

"Are you going back to bed?" Carlotta asked.

"Nope. Too tired to move. See you in the morning."

"G'night." Carlotta grabbed a cup and watered her houseplants. Mary, Jane, Lydia, and Kitty looked the same, as did Elizabeth. The Christmas cactus still lacked blooms. Carlotta moved it closer to the window and folded her arms. Maybe the plant's failure to bloom wasn't her fault. Maybe it was Jake preventing her from giving it so much light.

Carlotta had forgotten to tell her sister about the notes from Jake. But it wasn't the right time. Maybe when Rosario felt better. Her sister had been on edge since she'd read in the paper that a local college student had gone missing.

Jake knew Carlotta read the paper and would know about the missing woman. Could he be trying to play off her fears? Maybe that was his motive for sending the notes. But why would he do that? This was the man she'd spent a good portion of her life with. Was he trying to scare her into running back into his arms? It didn't make much sense.

Who else could have sent the notes? Carlotta willed her mind not to go there. Everything happened for a reason. Rosario needed her help. Carlotta picked up a romance novel. Perhaps she could play matchmaker between Pablo and her sister.

Someone in the family deserved a happy ending, even if it would not be her.

~*~

Jake knocked on the door to Rosario's place and noted the horseshoe that hung on it. Still superstitious. He didn't place much faith in luck. What did he believe in?

Rosario answered the door. So much for wishing she'd already be at work this Saturday so he wouldn't have to talk to her.

"He's here." She opened the door but stepped in front of Jake as he came closer and shoved her finger in his face. "Don't hurt my sister...any more than you already have."

He gritted his teeth. "It's nice to see you, too, Rosario."

Lopez women. As tough as they came. He'd initially admired that about Carlotta, though over time, it became clear the toughness was a façade.

Carlotta sat on the couch.

Jake lounged on the chair. He leaned toward Carlotta and fought back the urge to pull her into his arms. "How have you been? I've missed you. You could move back in. I could sleep in the guest bedroom."

She shifted her gaze away from him. "I thought

this was purely business."

"It…it is."

"Well, then, let's get to business."

"I heard the guy from the library had an alibi the night of the break-in."

She stared off into the distance. "Maybe one of his friends did it?"

Maybe he shouldn't have told her. Now, she'd only worry. Jake retrieved his cell phone from his pocket and opened the notes app. "Tell me about the night of the break-in."

"I went to the animal shelter. The dogs…" She clasped her mouth.

He reached for her hand. "We can stop for a moment if you'd like."

She pulled back her hand, a pained expression on her face. "No. Let's get on with this. I arrived at the animal shelter at six. I saw the dogs. I saw Ed. Then Geoffrey, um, Mr. Walters, was at the door. Then the police came…"

Jake jotted a note. "Wait, you mentioned the name Geoffrey. Was he there that night? I don't think I know him. Is he a friend from work?"

She scooted away. "Just like you have many, many female friends, I have male friends."

His chin dipped down. *Ouch.* "Fair enough. Your friend just happened to be there?"

She put a hand to her forehead and sighed. "Stick to the story, Jake."

Report the facts, but don't show bias. Easy to say when it didn't involve your wife. "But he was there, right?"

"Yes."

"Well, then I'm saying it's interesting, coincidental perhaps, that he showed up right then. Do the police know about this?"

"Yes, of course. The officer who showed up that night—I bet she can give you the full scoop. Undercover exclusive. After all, what you do now is your business." She covered her face with her hands.

Jake lowered his voice. "Kelsey—Detective Krouse—is only a friend. I haven't seen anyone else, and I don't *plan* on seeing anyone else." He leaned closer. If only things were as easy as kissing and making up.

"You're not sleeping with the blonde from work? Did she cheat on you?"

"I made a mistake. I admit it."

"Yes, you did." She pointed to the door, her chin quivered. "Please leave, Jake."

8

Settled onto his sofa, Jake tossed the divorce papers on the coffee table and cradled his head with his hands. One stupid mistake. This is what it might cost him. If he'd only gone to counseling. If he'd only told Carlotta how he felt, what was going on inside his head.

No, Carlotta couldn't have listened. She was too far gone with her own problems. Still, there had to have been a better way. Counseling, maybe. Although, it kind of felt like the thing weak people did.

He glanced at Carlotta's usual spot at their dining table. Had he taken control too many times? She'd been hurting. Meanwhile, 'fix things and move on' had been his motto. *I'm an idiot.*

He fed Gracie and then cleaned out the litter box. She'd learned how to use it quickly. Smart little creature.

The phone rang. He let it go to voicemail, and then picked up the manila package she'd sent him. Inside were her wedding rings. Jake studied the engagement ring. He'd had Carly and Jake inscribed on the inside. All the long hours of overtime and an extra job to pay for it. Nothing but the best for the finest girl.

He played with his wedding band. The cool metal

slid against his fingers. Jake fought the urge to rip off the band and toss it across the room. No, he would not give up that easily. She might have, but he wouldn't.

Jake stole a glance at the men's church retreat flyer on the couch cushion. Perhaps this would be the answer. Maybe the pastor could help him gain perspective, show him how to win back Carlotta. He could go to counseling, discuss fertility treatments, whatever she wanted. He had to get her back.

The phone rang

"Hello?"

"Jake, this is Stu. The mail room received another strange package, so the police will stop by to check things out. And I got a call from Human Resources. Allison Console has accused you of sexual harassment. I wanted to let you know because you and I have to sit down with HR tomorrow. You'll need to be in my office at 8:00 AM sharp."

"What? Stu, c'mon. You know me. The only thing I'm guilty of is stupidity." He sighed. "I slept with her. And believe me, anything that happened was consensual. She invited me to drinks and…" He couldn't remember much other than Allison seemed OK when they woke up together, certainly not accusing him of harassment at the time. An icy shiver… Yet he couldn't recall large portions of the evening. Perhaps that was a blessing.

"I believe you, kid, but apparently, she's telling everyone a different story. Says you verbally harassed her after you broke up. So we'll have to deal with that. See you tomorrow at 8:00 AM. And whatever you do, for goodness' sakes, don't wear plaid."

Jake hung up and headed to the bathroom. He splashed water on his face and fixed his gaze on the dark circles under his eyes as he tugged on his pants. Getting looser by the minute.

He grabbed yesterday's mail and sat on the couch. His leg shook. Maybe a quick trip to a casino might help him relax. Casting a glance at Granny's photo on the mantel, he took a deep breath and shifted his attention to the mail. Two flyers from local businesses. More junk mail. A bill. Ugh.

Jake got the checkbook, and his shoulders tensed. Would Carlotta ask for the house? He massaged a knot forming in his left shoulder. Might Carlotta remarry? And who was Geoffrey? Exactly how much of a friend was he? He cracked his knuckles. He loved Carlotta. He sure had a lousy way of showing it, but he did love her. That night had been what it was, a misguided attempt to deal with his pain. Allison meant nothing to him.

~*~

Carlotta watered her Christmas cactus. Poor Elizabeth's leaves had turned a light brown. Perhaps trauma from moving to a different location. She threw a hand to her forehead. Mrs. Macmillan! Carlotta had almost forgotten to water the neighbor's plants. She'd go over there later. Maybe after she walked the other neighbor's dog. Jake said she should say no sometimes. And yet how could she? He was going places with his job, always busy. Her heart felt empty. Doing things gave her importance.

Carlotta perused the newspaper, careful to avoid any stories Jake had written. She turned the page and did a double take. Two more missing women in the tri-state area. What was going on? Hadn't someone tried to kidnap a female jogger recently, too? What if someone had seen her at the animal shelter and had been waiting for her, and Ed was in the way and got killed as a result?

Rosario entered the kitchen.

Carlotta closed the newspaper. "So, what did the doctor say?"

Her sister grabbed a mug from a kitchen cabinet. "Last time, he performed an ultrasound. Today, he said my gallbladder looks fine. No problems there. Instead, he says I have irritable bowel syndrome. That's why I feel bloated all the time."

Carlotta pinched the skin at her throat. "Well, that explains the diarrhea, but what about the vomiting?"

Rosario filled the mug with water and heated it in the microwave. "He says sometimes that happens."

Carlotta drew her eyebrows together. So this would be a regular thing. How would Rosario manage this condition, go to work, and raise a child by herself? "Did he give you some medicine?"

The microwave beeped. Rosario removed the mug, added a tea bag, and steeped it. "I wish. Nope, he gave me this new diet instead. A list of foods I'm supposed to avoid for six weeks. Then I have to start slowly adding them back to my diet. It's to help me see what's causing the problem."

"So it's a food allergy."

Rosario joined Carlotta at the table. "He called it food intolerance. I think it's different." She retrieved a paper from the counter and sat back down. "Here. Do you want to read the paper he gave me?"

Carlotta studied the sheet. "Yikes, this list includes tons of different foods. Is there anything you *can* eat?"

Rosario sipped her tea. "I know. That's what I thought too. But if it helps me feel better, it's worth it. At least it's not something worse."

Remember how Tia Margarita had fought breast cancer. An awful end to such a beautiful life. "That's for sure. I was a little worried about you."

But what if the doctor had been wrong, and Rosario had something else? Cancer, perhaps? Who would raise Antonio then?

Jake cheated on her, and now this. She couldn't lose her sister, either. What were the odds of both things happening? Lots of bad things happened to the characters in the novels she read. Tons of conflict. Yet things managed to turn out. But what if this proved to be a horror story instead? Then what?

~*~

Jake had survived the morning meeting with HR. He couldn't remember much about the night with Allison, but he'd told the truth about what he knew and what happened afterward, and that was the most important part.

He now stood in front of the door to Matt and Marsha Stone's home, a large newer house in one of the northern suburbs. Manicured topiaries adorned either side of the doorway. He rapped on the door.

A man opened the door, presumably Mr. Stone. "May I help you?"

"I'm Jake Hartman. I'm with the local newspaper. I'd like to speak with your family. I wanted to do a write-up on the three missing college students, including Brittany. Maybe someone will see their pictures, remember something, and come forward."

"Come in."

Jake followed the man into the living room. The scent of apple cinnamon filled the room.

"Have a seat." The man gestured to a couch nearby.

"Thank you for talking with me." Jake sat.

The man's shoulders drooped. "I don't want her to be forgotten. Brittany is my oldest."

Jake gave an understanding nod. "Tell me more about her."

"She's a student over at the community college in the middle of town. Majoring in exercise science. She plays volleyball and softball." Mr. Stone blew out a breath. "If she hadn't gone to that party…"

A young blonde in shorts and t-shirt came down a flight of stairs nearby. "Hey, Dad. What's up?"

"This is a news reporter. He's here to talk to us about…" Mr. Stone's voice cracked, "Brittany."

"Arnold. Who's there? Come here," a female called from another part of the house.

The young woman plopped onto a chair near Jake. "I'm Madison. I'm a senior in high school."

"Can you tell me more about your sister?"

"She was…" Madison turned her head away. "Great. The best. She was…"

Jake raised a brow. "Was? Do you have reason to think she's no longer alive?"

"I'm hoping she'd be found by now, but three girls have gone missing. Like Dad said, maybe if Brittany hadn't gone to that party." Madison grimaced.

"Did she tell you about it?"

Madison looked at Jake, then away. "Her friends said there was alcohol there. She had some drinks. Someone could have slipped something in her tacos or drink."

Jake tilted his head. "Her tacos?"

"Yeah, you know those walking tacos, they…" Madison's chin trembled. She clasped her hand to her mouth.

"Is something wrong?"

Madison's eyebrows squeezed together. "I was there, too. My parents don't know. I'm underage. If they find out, especially my Mom, I'm dead. I want Brittany to be found as much as anyone. I was there with her and her friends. So it's not like telling anyone I was there would do any good anyway."

A petite, short-haired woman in a bright blouse and khaki pants barged into the room. Her high heels clacked against the floor. "Get out!"

Mr. Stone followed close behind. "Marsha. Wait!"

Jake stood.

Marsha looked at Madison. "Don't say another word. We're not talking to this man. Reporters always try to blame the victim."

A pinched expression spread across Madison's face. "But Mom…"

"Not. Another. Word." Marsha gritted her teeth and pointed toward the door. "Get out!"

"Thank you for your time." Jake hurried to the door and closed it behind him.

As he walked to his car, he blew out a breath.

He settled into the driver's seat. Only a few more stops. The college campuses. Three women attending three different institutions of higher learning. No common majors or extra curriculars. He huffed, pulled out of the driveway, and headed toward his next stop.

~*~

Jake parked in the visitor lot of Tonya Miller's college. He wouldn't dare go near Brittany Stone's college. He'd mention her name in his article. That'd be all.

With a quick glance, Jake double-checked the building sign against what he'd written down. Yep. This was the one. He meandered inside and located the women's basketball coach's office. He knocked on the door. A tall, thin woman in a t-shirt and shorts answered. A whistle hung around her neck, and she held a clipboard in her hand. "You're the reporter?"

He nodded.

"Follow me."

Jake jogged to keep up with the woman as she headed down the hall and turned into a gymnasium. A musty odor filled the air. Several girls set cross-legged on the wooden floor.

The woman stood in front of them. "This is Mr. Hartman. He's with the newspaper. He'd like to talk to you about Tonya." The woman looked down and walked to the nearby bleachers and sat, engrossed in her clipboard.

Jake moved toward the ladies. "Hi, you don't have to talk if you don't want to, but I'd like to do a story on all three missing students. If you'd like to talk, I'd appreciate it. They're missing right now, but maybe we can tell their story for them."

Several girls got up and walked over to the coach. She pointed to some basketballs on the other side of the gym. The women ran toward the other side and picked up balls and performed drills.

Three girls remained. The tallest spoke up. "We went to a party. We ate, and then… It was my fault."

A girl in a pink shirt to her right shoved her arm. "Stop that. It's not your fault. Quit saying that. You didn't do anything."

The tall girl shook her head. "If I hadn't eaten so much and gotten sick, then I wouldn't have had to run to the bathroom and left her alone."

A curly-headed girl to her left rolled her eyes. "You know you can't eat spicy food."

Pinkie leaned forward. "Tonya was a good player. She was our point guard. She was good on defense. She…."

Tall girl spoke up. "Was a great friend."

Curly nodded. "Yeah." She showed Jake a photo on her phone. "This is of us the weekend before." She pointed to a woman on the far right of the picture. "That's Tonya." She sniffed.

"Would you be willing to send me a copy of that photo?"

"Sure," Pinkie said.

Jake handed a business card to the woman. He pointed to the bottom. "Here's my e-mail address and cell phone. You can e-mail or text me the photo."

Jazz music filled the air. "Hold on one moment. I have to take this."

Jake held his phone and turned away. "Hello?"

"It's Stu. Where are you? You're supposed to be covering the boat show downtown and covering the bank robbery from last night."

Jake rubbed the back of his neck. "I'm over at the college…"

"Well what are you doing there?"

"I wanted to do a write up on the missing women."

"You're a reporter not a detective. Hurry up and get over to downtown. Then later head to the bank."

"Yes, sir." Jake hung up and turned to the ladies. "I'm sorry, but I have to go. Thank you for your time.

What if in his hurry, he'd missed something, important information that might lead to the girls? This was more than the story. This involved real people and their lives.

He huffed. Then again, maybe Stu was right. The

police had interviewed everyone. Not as if he'd uncover anything they hadn't.

~*~

Carlotta glanced outside at the gray clouds framing the horizon, and then re-joined Rosario and Antonio at the dinner table. "Going to be stormy tonight."

Rosario leaned toward Antonio and wiped his mouth. "No biggie," she smiled. "Mommy has flashlights and batteries."

"You're sure in a good mood. Been feeling better?"

"Yes, I've been trying to follow that diet the doctor gave me. And these." Rosario plopped a bottle of pills on the table. "One of our regular customers at work is a nutritionist. He recommended these. He said some people have digestive upset from low levels of stomach acid. Thought I'd try it. Plus, I picked up another lucky rabbit's foot."

Ugh. Her sister and her superstitions. Carlotta stabbed a piece of meat on her plate. "Should you ask your doctor first about taking those pills?"

Rosario smiled. "I'll be fine, Mom. But thank you for caring."

After dinner, Carlotta helped Rosario do the dishes.

Rosario then played with Antonio.

The wind howled. Tree branches scratched against the living room window.

"Where do you keep those flashlights? I can get

them in case we need them. You stay here with Antonio."

"In the cupboard next to the bathroom."

Carlotta went to the cabinet and pushed aside a box. Two flashlights worked. She headed down the hall. "I'll make fresh coffee. Want some?"

"Sure."

A few minutes later, the sounds of coffee percolating competed with the blare of a tornado siren.

Carlotta rushed into the other room. "Is that what I think it is?"

Rosario lowered her voice. "Yes, and stop it. Or you'll scare him. I forgot how frightened you used to get. It's only a storm, Carlotta. This isn't about this storm, is it?"

Tornados didn't induce panic in Rosario. They grew up in the same dysfunctional family, rife with alcoholism and codependency, and yet, they reacted differently. She had her fears, and Rosario had her superstitions. Carlotta lowered her volume to match Rosario's. "There's no basement. Where do we go?"

Rosario grabbed Antonio's hand. "C'mon, buddy. Let's go to the bathroom. We'll pretend we're camping in there."

Her sister acted like a natural with kids. Was this why Carlotta didn't have any? Was God merely sparing her? Carlotta bent down and grabbed one of Antonio's books. "I'll get the flashlights." She jogged to the kitchen, retrieved the flashlights, and met Rosario in the bathroom. "Here, buddy." She handed Antonio a small board book with a fuzzy bear on the front.

"Thanks for grabbing his book."

"You're welcome." Carlotta handed Rosario a flashlight and gripped the other with sweaty palms. She managed a slight smile at Antonio and then drew in deep breaths.

Rosario leaned in closer and touched Carlotta's shoulder. "Mom wouldn't go with you, would she?"

The wind howled. The tornado siren continued. How long would this go on?

Her sister moved to face her. "Dad was working, wasn't he?"

Carlotta chewed a nail. "Mom was....sleeping."

Rosario pursed her lips. "You mean drunk."

Looking downward, Carlotta wrapped her arms around herself. "I'd kept you busy by turning on the TV. You were hungry, so I went to the kitchen, and I found some peanut butter and spread it on some crackers. I gave them to you."

"Then the siren went off. I was scared."

Carlotta rubbed her eye.

"So you took me to the basement. I remember it was cold, and I didn't want to go down there. I asked you about Mom."

Carlotta's body trembled. "You wanted me to get her, and I tried. But she was passed out. I...I couldn't wake her. I was afraid she'd die. We were both just kids. I didn't know what to do."

Rosario lowered her voice. "Yeah, but you held my hand. You took me downstairs and comforted me."

Carlotta came closer and brushed her sister's hair out of her eyes. She bit back a whimper.

Rosario choked up. "Whenever she was passed out, you'd hold me, rock me, and tell it'd be OK." Recognition flashed in her eyes. "You had to be the parent, the adult in charge."

Carlotta nodded. Doing things for others, taking care of them. That's what she did. Putting others first. And besides, who didn't want to be needed?

Where was Jake? Was he OK? Whenever a tornado siren sounded, he'd go into the basement with her. He'd hold her in his arms, and the tension would melt away. If he was at work when a siren sounded, he'd call her. Always.

She retrieved her phone from her pocket and was about to call him. Her phone displayed several text messages and missed calls from him. Was it possible he still cared? Her heart skipped a beat. It wasn't too late to tear up the divorce papers. Yeah, but Rosario would chide her for backing down. Yet she'd stayed married to Pablo. What if Carlotta and Jake remained separated. He might change. She slumped her shoulders. *Remember Mom. Did she ever change?*

"Are you calling Jake?" Rosario huffed.

"I noticed I had some messages and calls from him."

Rosario rolled her eyes. "Don't worry. I'm sure he's safely snuggled up with his coworker." Her sister snatched the phone from Carlotta.

"What are you doing?"

"Helping." Rosario deleted the text messages from Jake and handed the phone back.

Heat flushed through Carlotta's body. "Why'd

you do that?"

Thunder rumbled.

She practiced deep breathing exercises for several minutes and then grabbed her phone. No new messages from Jake. Maybe Rosario was right. Perhaps he was too busy in the arms of a younger woman.

~*~

Jake gazed at the unlit street light outside his bedroom and then tried the landline phone. No dial tone. The storm had ended, but he needed to find out if Carlotta was OK.

As he walked about in the dark, he tripped and fell, hitting his head on the bed frame. Using the mattress for leverage, he stood. He couldn't tell if his vision was impaired by the bump or the dark. He held onto the wooden frame and went to the nightstand to find his cell phone. Wait a minute. Wrong side.

Putting his hand back on the bed, he wobbled around to the other side. His fingers bumped into the cell phone and knocked it to the floor. Jake picked it up and hit the power button. The display lit up, but the screen was damaged.

Now what? Would that guy...what was his name...call Carlotta and check on her? Bile rose in Jake's throat. He clenched his fists.

Jake stumbled to the stairs and then tripped on his way down. Pain seared through his body. He was in no shape to drive to see his wife at the moment.

"Is this what you want, God? I'm her husband. I

need to check on her. Do you hear me?" Jake shook his fist at the sky and then slumped back and rested on the floor. He'd run out of energy trying to rewrite this story.

~*~

After work, Carlotta entered the all-natural grocery store in Oakley close to the library.

She scanned her cart. Lactose free milk, veggies, and gluten-free bread. She headed for the self-checkout. Rosario's doctor had limited her diet, so Carlotta had offered to pick up some things.

"Carlotta?" a man asked.

She looked up from her cart. A well-dressed man with a basket approached. "Oliver? What are you doing here?"

He smiled. "I'm in town on business."

I don't want to hold up the line. She glanced behind them. No one else was waiting. "Oh, I thought your park was in Dayton." *Ugh. Why'd I say that?* Now he'd know she'd read about him. Might make him think she was interested in him.

"It is, but I'm consulting with other businesses that want to install zip lines. Plus, I'm thinking about expanding my operation to more than one location. Several eco parks throughout Ohio." He lifted an eyebrow. "How did you know I was in Dayton?"

She scanned the milk. "I read an article about you in a magazine at the library. I work there, you know."

"I'm surprised Jake didn't have a fit."

Carlotta averted her gaze.

Oliver stepped closer to grab her hand. "I see you're not wearing a ring. Are you still with Jake?"

"We're getting a divorce."

"I'm sorry to hear that."

She scanned the gluten-free bread. "No, you're not. You were mad at Jake when he and I got engaged."

Oliver scowled. Maybe she shouldn't have said that.

Gritting his teeth, Oliver lowered his voice. "He wasn't the only one I was mad at."

As she scanned her veggies, she shivered. No, he couldn't have been the one at the animal shelter. It had to be someone connected to Xavier.

Oliver flashed a smile. "But I couldn't stay mad at you for long, right?"

She nodded. That was why she'd broken off things with him. He did have quite a temper. She bagged her groceries.

He scanned the two items he had. "It's late. Why don't I walk you to your car?"

She set her bags in the cart. "I'm fine."

"Nonsense. It isn't safe to walk alone at night. It's not a problem." Tossing his items into a sack, he followed her.

She was walking with him whether she liked it or not. *Should I run or walk back to my car?* Carlotta gripped her key fob in her hand. Hitting the panic button was always an option. Her heart sank. The batteries had gone dead on the fob. Jake was supposed to order her new ones but forgot. She clenched her keys. If things went sideways, she could use them as a weapon. Carlotta scanned the parking lot for other patrons, anyone who might hear a potential cry for help. One person was several car aisles away. But still someone. Better than no one. Stopping in front of her car, Carlotta whipped around to face Oliver.

He took a step backward. "G'night. It was nice seeing you." He waved and strolled away. "You should come visit my park sometime. My parents still talk about you."

After locking the door, she sat for a moment. A note was tucked in the windshield wiper. She darted outside, grabbed it, and got back inside.

You're important to me.

You're special.

I couldn't do what I do without you.

Special? Her hands shook. Do what without her?

The animal shelter. Then Xavier in the elevator. Now these notes. She balled up the paper, rolled down the window, and tossed it into a trashcan next to the cart return.

Carlotta sped away even as she choked back a sob. Why fight it anymore? She'd had enough. A few minutes later, she pulled into Rosario's driveway. The note? What if the police could have dusted it for fingerprints? Why hadn't she thought of that before?

~*~

The long work week ended. Jake had signed up for

that men's retreat at church—only two hours away from home but in the great outdoors.

He drove home, captured Gracie with a handful of treats, and dropped her off at the kennel. Then he picked up a new cell phone and put it in the glove box. He clenched the steering wheel as he drove back to the house again.

At home he packed a suitcase and loaded it in the car. As he pulled out of the driveway, a black car followed. The car sped up, signaled, and then went around him.

Jake might enjoy some male bonding, reconnect with nature, and leave his woman troubles behind. Probably wiser than running off to the horse races or slot machines. It couldn't be worse than infertility testing and treatments. Funny how Carlotta talked about it as if it would help their marriage.

The car in front weaved around the semaphores at the railroad crossing, and then stalled. At least there wasn't a train coming.

Jake scanned his surroundings. No buildings for miles. Just trees and overgrown weeds. Good thing he was here. Not too many cars traveled this deserted, two-lane stretch. If he had to guess, it was probably a cell signal dead zone, too. Jake's gaze sharpened. Was that the same car from earlier this evening?

Jake got out. Gravel crunched beneath his tennis shoes.

The driver, a man with a black hoodie, put down his car window.

"You look like you're stuck, man," Jake said.

"How can I help?"

The man laughed.

Sudden pain on the back of his head, and then Jake sank into the darkness.

A whistle blared somewhere off in the distance.

Jake woke, groggy with confusion. The hard surface below him vibrated. His head ached, making it hard for him to open his eyes.

The blaring horn screeched with urgency.

Where was he?

Was that gravel and steel beneath him?

Jake pried open one eye.

A train went through a crossing.

He blinked. He'd been at that crossing. He blinked again. He was on the track. Jake scrambled to his feet and sprinted off the tracks.

The breeze of the train pushed Jake's hair and lifted his shirt. The conductor laid on the horn, almost as if admonishing Jake for the scare. Jake shook off his own fear. Adrenaline coursed through his body. He let out some deep breaths and then waited for the train to pass.

How had he gotten there? That motorist. Where was his car? The vehicle was parked off to the side of the road, nestled among overgrowth.

Jake patted his pockets. No car keys. His wallet was gone along with his credit cards, money, and license. He waded through tall weeds to get to the driver's side of his vehicle. The car door was open. He reached for the glove box. At least he still had a phone. Jake stuffed the phone into his pocket, got his suitcase, and started walking. Only a few more miles to the retreat. Stopping, he closed his eyes and tried to recall the license number. Maybe B5 something. Eventually, he'd need to report the attack. Right now, he just wanted to get to his destination.

Minutes later, a car pulled next to him. A man lowered his window. "You need a ride?"

Another car in the middle of nowhere. He hesitated. "Yeah. I got robbed. My car keys, cash, license, and credit cards were taken."

"Where are you headed?"

"To a men's retreat. It's near the old Boy Scout camp—"

"Then you're very fortunate. God put me here in the right place at the right time. My name is Bill Emery. I work at the retreat. I'm very sorry to hear someone robbed you. Don't worry about a thing. We'll get you set up in your room, and you can call the authorities and report your missing valuables."

"Thanks." Jake nodded. "I'm Jake Hartman."

"Good to meet you, despite the circumstances." Bill grinned.

When they arrived at the retreat, a man sat behind the counter, phone to his ear. He waved at Bill.

Bill stepped behind the front counter, entered some information into the computer, and handed Jake a key card.

Jake clenched the card. "Key cards?"

"We've updated our cabins."

Jake moved in the direction Bill indicated, strode into a bedroom, and slung his luggage onto the bed.

He gazed at the nightstand. A sound machine sat next to it along with a charging port for electronic devices. A modern cabin. Not what he expected from a church camp.

He spent the next few minutes on the cell phone getting his credit cards cancelled.

As soon as he hung up, a knock sounded. Jake opened the door, and a portly man ducked inside.

"Jake Hartman?" he asked with a Boston accent. "How are ya'? Looks like we'll be neighbors for the retreat. I'm Pastor Tom Clyde. Bob Hathaway asked me to come and speak to the group."

Jake shook hands with the man. "Nice to meet you." A chill in the air indicated the last occupant had left the air conditioning cranked up. He rubbed his arms.

"Do you know when we're eating?" the pastor asked.

"Why don't we head over to the supper hall right now?" Jake figured it couldn't hurt to check.

The two of them grabbed dinner, buffet style, then sat down at a table together.

"So what is your talk about?" Jake asked.

"Leadership."

Jake nodded blankly.

"Something else you'd rather talk about?"

"No, I'm good."

An hour later, Pastor Clyde went to the front of the large group and began his first talk of the retreat. He introduced himself, told a corny joke, and talked about King David of the Old Testament. The Bible referred to King David as a man after God's own heart. So pretty much nothing like Jake.

At the back of the room, Jake stood and eyed an exit. What was he doing here?

"And so David commits adultery with Bathsheba… Yep, the King sends out his men to war, and then he sees this woman bathing. He sleeps with her, and she sends word that she is pregnant."

Jake squeezed his eyes shut and sat back down. Ugh. What if that had happened to Allison?

"So David sends Uriah, Bathsheba's husband, to war, on the front lines, and then withdraws support, so the man will be killed," Pastor Clyde continued.

Yikes. Adultery and murder? Maybe not everyone in the Bible was a goody two-shoes after all.

"God sends the prophet Nathan, who tells David a story about a rich man who kills a poor man's lamb for food. David gets angry at the rich man in the story. Nathan essentially tells David, 'Hey, buddy, you're like the guy in the story.' Even great leaders make big mistakes, and if they repent, God can forgive. Tomorrow, we'll discuss the consequences of David's sin."

Forgiveness. Yeah, but unlike Jake, David was a Bible guy. Even if God forgave him, Pastor Clyde mentioned consequences. What if Carlotta divorcing him was one of those? Not to mention, him losing his job over the sexual harassment claim trumped up by Allison. Or what if Allison got pregnant?

Jake hurried back to the room.

Someone knocked on the door.

He opened it.

Pastor Clyde stared back at him. "You left there in a hurry. Are you OK?"

Jake motioned for the man to come inside. The pastor sat on a chair. Jake sat on the edge of the bed. He buried his head in his hands and sighed. Then he looked up at the pastor. "My wife filed for divorce. It's my fault. I was like David. I messed up. As my principal would say, I deserve what I get. You know, the consequences. I guess I've lost Carlotta for good."

The pastor lowered his voice. "We all deserve hell, but God provided a way around that. Yeah, there will be consequences, but you and I don't know what they are."

Jake nodded politely. What was the pastor trying to communicate? How did this relate to his marriage?

"Don't give up on your wife. If your divorce isn't final, there's still time for you to fight for your marriage. Go after her."

Yeah. He'd win her back. As with King David, there would be consequences, repercussions. He might lose his job, not much he could do. But he had to try to fix his marriage, had to fight for Carlotta.

~*~

Carlotta joined her sister in the living room and rested a hand on her shoulder. "You're doing the right thing."

Rosario stared off into space. "Am I?"

Carlotta couldn't fix her marriage, but maybe she

could encourage her sister to repair hers. It was worth a shot. Plus, helping people always made her feel good. And certainly, that ought to please God, right? So maybe she didn't always enjoy doing it, but she did it anyway. Mom would be drunk. Dad coped by seeing women from work. Rosario acted out. And Carlotta did good deeds. Yep, her worth came from doing. Was that all she had going for her? A bothersome feeling overcame her, but she pushed it aside. "You need a break, and Antonio needs some time with his father."

A car pulled into the driveway.

Carlotta stood. "That's him. Do you want to get the door, or should I?"

Rosario stared at nothing in particular.

She waved her hand in front of her sister's face. "Hello? Rosario? Should I get that?"

Her sister flinched. "No, I will." Rosario opened the door.

Pablo smiled. "Hi, Rosario, Carlotta."

"Hi, Pablo." Carlotta headed toward the bedrooms.

"Wait" Rosario pinched her chin. "Please stay."

Carlotta glanced at her watch. She still needed to go to the bank and the post office. But her sister needed her. She sank into the couch, and Pablo joined her.

Rosario sat in a chair. "Can you watch Antonio for me?"

Carlotta could have watched him, too. But maybe Rosario preferred someone with more parenting experience. Not that Pablo had much of that. She bit her nail.

"Yeah, sure." Pablo rubbed his lips. "Everything OK, Rosie?"

"I've been a little sick lately. No big deal. Can you watch him or not?"

"Yeah, sure. Let me know whenever you need my help. Just give me a heads up so I can ask off from work."

"You're working?" Rosario's voice rose in pitch. "Like legit?"

"I told you. I've been clean from drugs for over a year."

No more needle marks. Normal-looking pupils. Changed demeanor and apparel. While looks could deceive, if Pablo was aiming to defraud, he was doing a pretty good job. From all external appearances, Carlotta's brother-in-law seemed as though he hadn't been using for quite some time.

"I have a job," Pablo continued. "I go to church. Got Jesus. Found my worth in Christ. The real deal, Rosie."

Carlotta tilted her head. His worth in Christ? Oh, like helping at church and stuff. What else could he mean?

"OK. Thank you." Rosario walked Pablo to the door.

Once Pablo left, Carlotta pressed a fist to her mouth. "I can't believe how much he's changed."

Rosario shrugged. "A lot of 'em find God in prison, Carlotta. The question is, can they keep Him once they get out?"

~*~

Jake yawned as he followed Pastor Clyde outside.

"Ready to go on that zip line?" the man asked.

Just what he needed. The thrill, the rush, and a distraction from his separation from Carlotta and the accusations by Allison. "Uh. Yeah."

Jake and Pastor Clyde approached the zip line tower and ascended the stairs.

Pastor Clyde huffed as they climbed. "A bit of a workout, eh?"

Jake chuckled.

As they stopped at the top, Jake surveyed the forest below. There was something about nature, like getting in touch with God. Maybe because out here, things were more still. More time for reflection on life. He stepped toward the attendant.

"Let me help you into the harness," the attendant said. The man had an accent, but Jake couldn't quite place it.

Jake stepped closer and followed the man's directions.

"Here's your helmet."

Jake snatched it from the attendant and put it on. "Thanks."

"You ready?"

"Sure." Jake clenched his fists.

The attendant performed one last safety check and explained what would happen.

Jake flew from the platform and zipped along the line. What a rush. He took in the scenery. Trees. A creek. More trees. A deer? No, a person? Maybe a camper? Hard to tell. His gaze shifted to the tower at the end of the line. Over already? He'd have to ride again.

Several of the men had hurried over to the crossbow station, leaving the line short. Jake took another turn on the zip line. The object he'd seen before was no longer in sight. Just trees and open skies. He took in a deep breath. Once he reached the other tower, the operator on that side helped him out of the harness.

Jake jogged down the stairs of the platform and trekked toward the cafeteria. They'd be eating soon. He meandered along the wooded trail, closing the distance between himself and the camp buildings. The smell of grilled meat filled the air. He'd glanced at the menu earlier. Brats for dinner. He licked his lips.

The dinner bell clanged in the distance. He couldn't see it, but he'd noticed it earlier that morning. It set outside the cafeteria, an older style, like the ones used years ago.

Several larger trees framed the path up ahead. As he walked through the tree grove, burning pain shot through his left calf.

The bell clanged again.

"Yeowch!" Jake stumbled and bent down on his hands and knees. His lower left leg flamed with burning pain. An arrow stuck out the back. "Stop! I've been hit!" he yelled.

His voice competed with the clanging of the dinner bell.

Someone had goofed up big time. Only one area was for shooting, and that was at the crossbow range. What if the shooter didn't hear him? He limped behind a tree, blowing out short breaths as pain radiated up his leg.

Third clang. Earlier, the staff had rung the bell five times. Maybe then someone could hear him and get help.

Clang!

He didn't see anyone. Maybe they were embarrassed and took off, or perhaps they hadn't seen or heard him.

Clang! Last one.

"Help! I've been hit!"

The tower operator popped out of the woods and ran toward Jake. "What happened?"

"I got…hit by a…stray arrow." Jake had to unclench his teeth to talk.

"Ugh. They shouldn't be shooting over here." The man grabbed his walkie talkie and radioed for help. "The retreat nurse will be here shortly. She'll call 9-1-1."

"Ah!" Pain seared through his flesh. He grabbed his leg and winced. As he turned around to sit upright, he bumped the end of the arrow. It moved slightly. "Ahhhh!"

The operator grimaced. "I'm so sorry. I wish I could do something more for you, but I can't remove it."

"I under….stand…" Jake groaned.

"We've had to chase a few men away from this

area, but we've been fortunate no one has been hit before. The regulars obey the rules, but sometimes they invite friends who aren't used to the retreat and our regulations."

Gosh, this guy was chatty, but he distracted Jake from the pain. A little.

Jake turned his head, careful not to move the arrow farther, and examined where the back of the arrow protruded from his leg. Blood trickled near the wound.

A woman dressed in a shirt with the camp logo on it sprinted toward them with a medical kit in one hand. "I heard there was an accident. I've called for help. The ambulance should be here shortly. I'll let them remove the arrow, but I'll try to stabilize it for now." She removed a pressure bandage from her first aid kit. "Would you like us to call anyone for you? Family?"

Carlotta flashed in his mind. "No. No, but thank you."

The woman applied the pressure bandage near the wound and then removed a roll of tape from her kit. "I'm going to tape the bandage and try to prevent the arrow from moving and causing any more damage." She looked at the zip line operator. "Can someone grab me another arrow? The doctor will want one for comparison."

Another man approached. "Hello, I'm the camp manager. We've never had this happen before. I'm so sorry. We're shutting down and roping off the crossbow station for now as a precaution."

"Accidents...ugh. Happen." Jake moaned.

A siren blared as the ambulance approached. The doors opened, and two paramedics exited. Using cutters, they shortened the end of the arrow and applied more bandaging to his leg.

Sweat beaded on his body as he held in a scream. Despite his efforts, a groan slipped out.

The zipline operator returned. The man stepped forward and handed one of the paramedics an arrow. "Here you go."

The paramedics removed a stretcher from the ambulance. Using care, they lifted Jake atop the stretcher and pushed him into the vehicle.

Jake took deep breaths, hoping to lessen the pain. It seemed to work a little.

"We'll get you fixed up," one of the paramedics said.

He blew out a breath. If only he could do the same with his marriage.

9

Jake sat up in the hospital bed and smoothed the sheets. He glanced at the bandage on his forearm where the IV had been located earlier. His mind flashed to the last time he'd been in the hospital...for a tonsillectomy. Dad was still alive. Somehow, the rooms seemed much simpler then. They'd treated his emergency without ID. He'd have to get replacement cards as soon as possible.

Officers from the local sheriff's department had visited his room right after surgery and collected the other half of the arrow. Jake had been rushed into the operating room before they could meet with him earlier. The deputies believed the incident to be accidental. No one had come forward to accept responsibility, but the arrow in his leg matched the ones used by the retreat. A very common style, the metal-tipped arrows were also used by another camp in the area, which adjoined the retreat he attended. Who knew from which spot the arrow had come from? Bottom line was he was OK now, and the pain killers and antibiotics were doing their job.

A young, red-headed nurse wearing bright scrubs checked his vitals. "The arrow hit the fleshy part of your leg and avoided the large vessels. No massive muscle damage. It should heal fairly quickly. Thankfully, you weren't hurt worse."

Jake glanced at the whiteboard on the wall, which listed the names of the doctor, nurse, and any other techs. "So, Angela, where are my things?"

"I'll get them." The nurse left the room.

Jake checked the display of his new cell phone. Three texts. He opened the first. Thank goodness the nurse left the room. Who sent these racy messages? The messages could be from Allison, but he had no proof. Maybe better to open the other two later.

Angela strode back with a bag of his belongings.

Jake massaged his temples and looked at the clock. "When do I get out of here?"

"The doctor wants to check on you, but hopefully this evening. We'll send you home with discharge information and a prescription for antibiotics. You're going to want to keep an eye on the wound and watch out for infection. If you have any questions, you can call the number on the paperwork."

Clenching his jaw, he said, "Lucky me."

"Could have been worse. Could have hit you in the head or the chest. Or hit a large vessel." Angela's chin trembled.

"Everything OK? I hope I didn't upset you."

"No, my boyfriend." The nurse shook her head, sniffing and wiping at her nose. "I apologize, you…"

"It's OK. Go ahead."

"My boyfriend came in here, but he never made it home. A drunk driver hit him while he rode his motorcycle." Angela clutched at a cross on her necklace.

"May I ask you a question?"

"Sure." The nurse continued to fidget with her necklace.

"Do you still believe in God?" Jake asked.

Angela nodded. "Yes, I'm a Christian."

"Why? God let a drunk driver kill your boyfriend. Aren't you angry?"

"You bet. It took me a while to forgive. But God forgave me of my sins. I had to forgive the drunk. I didn't want to become bitter. I don't like what happened, but it doesn't change the fact God's still in control." She sniffed and wiped her eyes. "Sometimes bad things happen to good people. I'm sure you'd agree."

Jake nodded. "Oh, yeah. I get paid to report on them."

"The man who hit Michael. What he did affected me, Michael, and his whole family..." A page came over the loudspeaker. "I have to go." Angela left the room.

Sin affected others. How had what Jake done affected Carlotta? As with King David, there were consequences. They'd broken up. She might divorce him. *If only I hadn't gone out with Allison that night...*

Jake checked his second message. From Pastor Clyde. Better return the call. "Hey, it's Jake. I'm at the hospital. I'm doing OK. Should get out of here this evening."

"I'm glad to hear that. The camp director wants to apologize."

He huffed. "Accidents happen."

"The crossbow station is fairly far away. Campers shouldn't be shooting arrows in that area. They're closing it down for a while, maybe even permanently. I'm so sorry."

Jake replayed the incident. That shadowy figure who'd been on the ground. A person, or merely an animal? Most likely nothing and wouldn't prove anything. Not as if he'd ID'd anyone. What about Oliver? Carlotta's ex? He had a motive. But why now? The guy lived in Dayton, and Carlotta hadn't seen him in years. He didn't need to mention any of his suspicions to the deputies. It'd just take up more of his time and theirs. They'd ruled it an accident, and that's what it'd been.

Probably a camper with bad aim, who was ashamed to come forward. Over the years, he'd reported on various crimes and accidents. His uncle would have connected the dots between all the bad incidents and tried to form some sort of theory. Rosario, on the other hand, would have chalked it up to bad luck. Nope, bad stuff happened. Life wasn't fair. End of story. "I'm fine. I won't sue or anything if that's what they're worried about."

"He simply wants to make sure you're doing OK and that no one else gets hurt."

"I understand."

"Do you want me to contact your wife? Let her know you're OK?"

"My wife?" He flinched. "No, not necessary. I'll see you around."

"I'm so thankful you're OK. It could have been worse. I'll pray for you. If there's anything else I can do for you, please don't hesitate to call."

His phone pinged again. Probably another awful text message. His shoulders slumped. Carlotta left him. Allison accused him of sexual harassment. His boss couldn't protect him anymore. He might lose his job. And now someone might be trying to kill him. Could it get worse? He'd written a lot of stories for the newspaper, but none like this one.

10

Monday morning, Jake reclined in his office chair and dialed Carlotta's work number. "Hi, Becca, this is Jake—"

"You?" she huffed. "Carlotta is busy."

So even her boss had relegated him to the doghouse. Talk about the cold shoulder. "I need to talk to her. It's urgent."

A long sigh sounded. "Have you left a message on her cell? I'd try that. If she doesn't respond, then obviously she doesn't want to speak with you. Now, if you'll excuse me, I'm busy."

The dial tone continued for a minute. Then Jake hung up and headed for the door.

At this hour, Carlotta had probably gone to lunch. Only one place she'd go.

Jake drove to the café on Red Bank Road near the post office. Pleasant-smelling, pink and red flowering bushes bloomed in front of the short brick building. Carlotta would know the name. She was so smart. Why hadn't he realized this before? But when did he lose sight of her, stop cherishing her? He shook his head.

He stumbled inside and scanned the aging, remodeled building. No sign of her. A door off to the right led outside to a separate eating area. Another patron came by and opened the door. Jake trudged inside. Carlotta sat off to the left at a wrought iron bistro table with a red patio umbrella. She was there with…some guy. Already? And one much younger. He nodded his head. Had to be a coworker, another librarian. Her supervisor often volunteered her to train new hires. He shouldn't jump to conclusions.

Then again, the way he leaned in toward her, looked at her. Jake blinked rapidly.

Carlotta spoke, and the man chuckled and moved closer to her.

Jake stepped toward the couple and cleared his throat. "Carlotta, may I have a word with you?"

She gasped and stared at the bandage on his leg. "You're hurt."

The mystery man avoided eye contact.

Jake clutched his fists at his sides. Now if he could only tame his tongue. "We need to talk now."

"I'm having lunch with a friend. Can I call you later?" She lifted a brow. "Besides, shouldn't you be getting back to work?"

Jake chuckled.

"What's so funny?" Carlotta asked. She turned her chair toward him and away from the other man. A step in the right direction.

Leaning closer, he said, "I'm on probation."

"Probation?" She smirked and then cleared her throat. "For what?"

He averted his gaze. "It's complicated."

"Someone suing the paper over something you

wrote?"

Traffic roared in the distance, yet he lowered his voice. "I had my second meeting with Human Resources this morning. Allison has accused me of," he took a deep breath, "sexual harassment."

Carlotta laughed. "It's not funny, but I've seen her. Seems to me as if she's the one who'd do the harassing. Though rough around the edges, Stu is a good man. He'll believe you if you just tell him what happened."

"Stu may not have a say. He's getting pressure from up above. If push comes to shove, I'm gone." Kind of like what happened in his marriage.

"Can they do that without proof?"

"The company will do what's best for them."

Carlotta leaned toward him and then pulled away. "What happened to your leg?"

"Got hit by an arrow at a retreat." He shrugged.

She gasped. A look of concern spread across her face.

He raised a hand. "I'm fine."

Carlotta's male friend cleared his throat and stood. "I should be going."

After turning toward the man, she touched his arm. "Wait, Geoffrey. Don't leave. We can discuss this later, Jake. Please, let us finish our lunch."

Us. Ouch. It must be time to buy a big old mop to clean up this mess. Now to find out where to get one that size.

~*~

Carlotta had never seen Jake so angry. But he was the one who had committed adultery. She clenched and then relaxed her fists. What was it that a coworker had once told her? Divorce was like a death. Oh, well, time to go to work and to push conflicting feelings aside.

Rosario came into the kitchen. "I have to drop off Antonio at Pablo's. He's watching him today. Wanna go with me, and we'll grab some breakfast at the drive thru while we're out?"

Carlotta cast a glance at her sister. "Yes, and I'm buying."

"OK, but I'm driving." Rosario grabbed her keys. "You OK with that?"

"Sure."

Rosario drove them several blocks away. As they passed windows with bars on them, Carlotta locked her door. A homeless man sat on the corner and stared. They neared Pablo's apartment. Two police cars surrounded Pablo's car. She shot a look at Rosario. "There must be a reasonable explanation." Could he really be using drugs again? What other reason could there be?

Her sister's mouth fell open. "There are cops by his car. I should have known it. Bad things always happen in threes. Ed died. I've been sick, and now this."

Some neighbors had gathered and were filming the scene on their cell phones.

Carlotta shook her head. What was wrong with people? She pointed. "There's Pablo. With handcuffs."

Not again, Pablo. I really thought you changed.

A stocky officer helped Pablo into the back of a police vehicle. Another, slimmer officer stood next to Pablo's car with the back door ajar.

Too bad Antonio had to see all this.

Rosario rubbed her temple. "What will I do? You have to work. The daycare is closed today." She handed her sister the keys. "Here, you drive. I don't feel so good."

Carlotta traded places with Rosario. As she drove away from Pablo's apartment complex, she glanced at her sister. "Who watched Antonio before Pablo?"

Rosario's eyes grew watery. "The older lady down the street. But she's gotten too old to watch him."

"You know, I have a coworker who's off today. Let me give her a call."

Rosario dipped her head. "Thank you."

"You're welcome."

Carlotta didn't rest until she'd located a sitter for Antonio. After getting breakfast for everyone, she dropped her sister at work and her nephew at the sitter's. She blew out a breath as she arrived at work. She shook her head as she walked into the library. Pablo really seemed as if he'd changed.

When it was break time, she picked up some children's books and movies for Antonio. After lunch, she went to the video section. She breezed by the romance section. Rosario didn't need that. Something funny. Yes, that should cheer up her sister a little.

At the end of the day, she packed up all her items and picked up her sister and nephew. On the way home, she let Antonio flip through one of the board books. Judging by the smile on his face, he enjoyed it.

When they got home, Carlotta pointed at her sister. "Go into the other room. Now."

"Huh?"

"I'm making dinner. Tamales. Just go and play with your son. I've got this." Carlotta winked at Rosario like when they were younger and it was the two of them against the rest of the world.

Rosario threw up her hands and grinned. "OK, OK."

Carlotta prepared the tamales. She and Antonio enjoyed the meal, but Rosario barely touched her food.

Carlotta gave Rosario a playful shove. "Go read with your son. I'll do the dishes."

After dinner, Rosario helped Antonio get ready for bed.

Carlotta made two cups of coffee and set them on the table.

Rosario joined her in the kitchen. "He's all tucked in."

"So the police caught Pablo with drugs, but he told the officer someone planted them on him?"

Rosario huffed. "Yeah, right. Once a user, always a user."

Carlotta's shoulders tightened. What if Pablo had something to do with Ed's death? Was it possible? He had been at Rosario's house the morning she found the roses. Pablo could have sent them and tried to make her think they'd come from Jake. Maybe she was overthinking things. Perhaps it was easier than blaming Jake for his actions. Her lips curled. *I wish I'd never encouraged Rosario to reconnect with Pablo.*

Carlotta's phone buzzed. An incoming message from Geoffrey.

It was nice he was calling, but right now, she'd rather talk to Jake. He'd always been a good listener when it came to discussing things. It was what made him a good reporter.

~*~

Jake went to the coffeemaker. Maybe he couldn't fix his marriage right now, but he could still try to look after his wife. Perhaps find out who was behind the attack at the animal shelter.

Randy joined him. "You're here early."

"With the storm last night, I got little sleep. I was already awake, so I came in. Plus, doing a little personal research. Been looking into the APCC. One member was recently released from prison. We might want to see if he's friends with this Xavier guy who's obsessed with Carlotta." Jake poured himself some coffee.

Randy poured a cup. "You still think they had something to do with the death at the animal shelter?"

He took a sip of his coffee. "Maybe. You remember the serial killer from Covington?" A dark case, one that gave him the chills.

"Who doesn't?" Randy sipped from his mug. Aliens adorned the side.

Jake poured his drink down the drain. "This latest

incident seems reminiscent of his work."

Randy continued to sip his coffee. "But it's not his usual MO, right?"

Ed's body appeared unharmed at the animal shelter—maybe he'd been smothered or poisoned. The dogs had been slashed, though. Inconsistent, very strange. But the serial killer, he'd been more brutal.

Jake took the coffeepot, dumped the old grounds in the trash, and carried the carafe to the sink. "No, but his killings were similar. Knife slayings. Same time of year, always at nonprofits. They stopped for ten years, but it could be he's up to his old tricks again. Maybe, unbeknownst to everyone, the police put the killer behind bars for something else, and now they've recently released him from prison. Able to go back to his old ways."

"Wait." Randy said. "Didn't the prime suspect in those cases die? Cancer, right?"

Carlotta would have to stop her nighttime volunteering. He'd have to put his foot down. It wasn't safe to be working alone late at night. "Lung cancer." Jake emptied the carafe, refilled it with fresh water, and then nodded. "Yep, but he left behind a son. One who defended his dad vehemently."

Randy leaned closer and quirked a brow. "The type who might take over in his father's footsteps? A copycat?"

"Or he wasn't the Covington killer, and the police had the wrong suspect. Anything is possible." Jake started a fresh pot of coffee. Stu could thank him later.

"Did he ever send pipe bombs?"

Jake glanced at his desk. Mounds of paperwork stared back at him.

What if the killer was targeting the newspaper? Wouldn't fit the Covington killer's MO, though. Not a nonprofit. "Don't think so." He sank into his chair. Thank goodness the package at his house had been harmless. Still, he was glad the police had checked it out.

The pipe bombs. The animal shelter. He sighed. No closer to solving this mystery than before.

11

It wasn't Easter, and it wasn't Christmas, and yet, Jake found himself in front of Cincinnati Evangelical Free Church. He went inside.

Today, he was at a church speaking with the pastor—an actual counseling session to try to make some sense of his relationship woes with Carlotta.

When an article had a problem, he edited it. He wasn't sure how to revise his marriage, but counseling was a good place to start.

He entered the church office. The secretary didn't look up right away. Maybe she'd heard about his infidelity. "I'm here to see Pastor Clyde. I have a lunchtime appointment."

She picked up her phone. "Mr. Hartman is here to see you." She nodded, hung up, and addressed Jake. "He's ready to see you. You may go in."

Jake entered the door and took a seat.

Pastor Clyde leaned across his desk. "Nice to see you, Jake. How's the leg?"

"It's getting better. It's fine."

"Glad to hear that. How's everything else?"

Jake ran his left thumb along the scratches in the guest chair. He shifted his gaze to Pastor Clyde's desk. Matching dents covered the surface of the furniture. A mega church this wasn't, but perhaps that was what had drawn him here. The humility of the place. "As I told you earlier, my wife and I have been having some problems. She wants a divorce."

"I see."

"It's not only that. We haven't been able to have children. And then I did something idiotic. I had a few drinks with a coworker, and I ended up sleeping with the woman. I apologized, but my wife wants nothing to do with me. I wondered what the Bible says about divorce. Sort of for my own curiosity, but also because my wife comes from a family that's a bit religious."

"And you? What's your religious background like?"

"Granny took me to church sometimes."

"God designed marriage to be a covenant. As Jesus said, in marriage, a man would leave his mother and father and cleave to his wife. By committing adultery, you've broken that covenant, Mr. Hartman."

Jake held his head in his hands. He didn't need a thesaurus to know what that meant. A promise, a pledge, a vow, a covenant. Sleeping with another woman who wasn't his wife. Yep, he'd broken it all right. "How can I fix it?" His breath caught in his chest. "*Can* I fix it?"

~*~

Jake stopped by the courthouse to pick up his brother-in-law. Had it only been a week or two since he'd called asking for help, saying someone had planted drugs on him?

Pablo trotted out of the courthouse with his lawyer and then hugged Jake. "Thanks, man."

"Thank the lawyer," Jake said. "She did all the work."

His brother-in-law turned to Gina Lampton, his defense attorney. "Thank you."

"You're welcome. Talk about a sloppy criminal. The man who planted the drugs on Pablo worked at the mechanic's garage where Pablo had taken his car recently to get the tail light fixed. The police found his fingerprints on the cardboard box and on the brake light, which someone had clearly tampered with. Needless to say, the man has drug-related prior offenses. Given his history, he'll probably bond out pretty quickly. Now, if you'll excuse me, I have another case to handle." Gina walked back inside the courthouse.

"Wow," Jake said, "I knew Gina worked fast, but that was pretty quick."

Jake glanced around and turned to get a better look.

Carlotta's friend Geoffrey walked by, same smarmy smile as before. Then again, the guy was just friends with Carlotta, just as Jake was with Detective Krouse. Perhaps he was reading too much into things.

A moment later, Pablo nodded his head in the man's direction. "That dude."

Jake shrugged. "The guy who's friends with Carlotta?"

Pablo's eyes widened. "Him?"

Jake rolled his eyes. "Yeah." A slight growl escaped his throat, and he clenched his teeth.

His brother-in-law narrowed his gaze. "I thought I saw him with the blonde you were seeing."

Jake folded his arms. "I'm not dating her. She's nothing but trouble. Let him get involved with her. Better him than me. Plus, maybe that will keep him away from my wife."

Nodding, Pablo grinned. "You do still love her."

He swallowed hard. "Of course, I do."

"Good, then let's get our wives back. You help me. I help you."

Pablo stared at Jake and hugged him again. "Given my past history, I didn't think anyone would believe me. I thank God for sending you to help me."

"Well, do me a favor. Can you see if He can send someone to help me with my life?" Jake grinned.

~*~

Jake's fingers swiftly moved along his keyboard. He paused and then cracked his knuckles. The words on the computer screen stared back at him. An article about Roman Collins. The guy who was accused of planting drugs on Pablo. He was out on bond awaiting trial when police found his body in the Ohio River.

Overcome by the sudden scent of incense, Jake turned around.

"What are you working on, dude?" Randy asked.

Jake closed his browser. His coworker stared at him from a nearby seat. "A little lunch time research.

Personal."

Lifting an eyebrow, Randy nodded. He raised a newspaper and pointed to a photo. "See this? The dude confessed to setting off the pipe bombs in our building."

"Good, I'm glad they caught him. Though I'm surprised he confessed."

Randy folded the newspaper. "I'm not. Considering two years ago, the same dude confessed to another crime."

"Oh?"

After setting the paper down, Randy folded his arms. "Claims he shot President Kennedy. Of course, he hadn't been born yet. The police released him, but they have another suspect. Apparently, a dude who used to clean our building but then was fired. His wife left him, and he became homeless."

Jake leaned closer. "So he's got a motive."

Randy nodded. "And a record. And he's a member of APCC—one group who had a beef against the animal shelter where your wife volunteered."

Jake crossed and then uncrossed his legs. "I looked into this patron who flirted with Carlotta and then later trapped her in the elevator. Xavier Paxton. He was adopted by a family member after his parents died when he was a teen. Ex-military. Loner. Still on the loose. Then there's Oliver Robertson. Into the environment. Zip lines. Kayaking. Crossbows. Archery. Don't know much about his early life history. His parents were wealthy. Maybe kept everything hush-hush on purpose. He was pretty ticked off when I stole Carlotta away from him. Considering I was injured by a stray arrow, well… Anyway, I suspect both to some degree, but I heard Xavier had an alibi for the night of the animal shelter incident. I'd assume Oliver does too, or else the police would haul them away by now. That and they have found no camera footage connecting either of them to the incident."

"Maybe. Or maybe they don't have enough evidence on them yet. Or maybe someone close to them is doing their dirty work." Randy narrowed his gaze. "What's eating at you?"

Huffing, Jake steepled his fingers. "You know those conspiracy theories you're into?"

Randy snorted and then let out a hearty laugh. "Which one?"

Leaning closer, Jake lowered his voice. "Can you help me find someone? Someone who doesn't want to be found?"

Randy inched closer. "Who is it?"

"Geoffrey Walters. He's an attorney. Been getting friendly with my wife."

"Dude, totally not cool."

"I've searched, and there's not much on him. His history only goes back three years."

Leaning back, Randy grinned. "A ghost. Sneeeeaky. I'll do it. On one condition."

"What's that?" Jake asked.

"Help me not to tick off Stu. 'Cause I'm dying here. I need to keep this job."

Jake opened a drawer and retrieved a paper from the bottom.

Randy skimmed it and chuckled. "No way, dude. You made an actual list of things our boss hates, stuff to avoid. You're the man."

At least one person thought so. Randy raised a hand to high five Jake.

Jake went back to work on his next article.

An hour later, Randy returned and dropped a paper on Jake's desk. "Shazam."

Jake picked up the paper. "What is this?"

His coworker gestured toward the document. "Name change. That's why you couldn't find the dude. Three years ago, he was Jeffery Barr."

"And what do we know about him?"

"Nothing yet. Gotta give me time, dude. I am good, but not that good." Randy adjusted his glasses. "You know, I got tickets for a tour of the Cincinnati Subway. We could grab some chili and tour the underground."

Jake poked his tongue against his cheek. "I thought they stopped giving those several years ago."

"They did. But with support from the new mayor, the city changed its mind."

"No, thanks. You'll have to find someone else to be your plus one." Jake winked.

~*~

The following evening, Randy stopped by Jake's desk. Jake glanced at the clock. Almost 5:00 PM. He relaxed his shoulders. "Touring the subway again?"

"Naw. C'mon, let's go to the casinos."

His stomach churned. Not the place for him. Besides, why should he share yet another indiscretion with a coworker? "OK." He could watch Randy play.

Jake rode with Randy to the casino. He took a deep breath and cracked his knuckles. He didn't have to gamble.

As they sat at the roulette table, Jake's gaze shifted to the other participants. Two men in suits—one of them in sunglasses—surrounded a pretty blonde in a silver cocktail dress who was turned to face an older gentleman behind them. As she moved around, he did a double take. Her eyes met his and lowered. Detective Krouse? This didn't seem like the sort of place she'd frequent. Then again, he didn't exactly need to be there either.

Randy leaned over and whispered. "You OK, dude?"

"Uh, yeah." He stared at Krouse, and the gentleman on her left glared, leaned forward, and moved his coat to reveal his pistol. So subtle a casino camera might not pick it up from that angle. But enough that he did.

Jake straightened his tie and drew in a quick breath. "I uh...I think maybe I'll play after all." Randy passed him some chips. "Here, I'll spot you. You can pay me back later. You know, when you hit the jackpot, dude."

Jake shook his head. "Thanks, but I got this." He stood and cast a glance at Krouse.

The man in sunglasses coughed loudly. What was his problem?

Could she be in trouble? He didn't want to leave her there. Should he call the police? Wait, they were already there. Hmm....maybe she was working undercover. Yeah, maybe that was it. Though she didn't make eye contact with him. Was that a distress signal, or was she trying not to blow her cover? Maybe he could call the police station.

Although where was Hadley? Shouldn't he be here, too, or another officer? The detectives didn't have partners, per se, but they'd work together when there had been a murder, or for arrests, or if backup was needed. He'd asked Krouse about it before. She'd lectured him about how crime shows on TV weren't like real life. Their department didn't have the staffing required to constantly pair up detectives. Yet in this instance, shouldn't she have some kind of backup? Jake got his chips and then paced the casino floor, even checking the restroom. No sign of the other detective anywhere.

Jake returned to the roulette table.

Randy quirked a brow. "What took you so long?"

Jake glanced at the ball bouncing around the roulette wheel. "I...uh. Had to use the bathroom."

His coworker chuckled.

Jake placed an inside bet on five. The day of his anniversary.

"Are you for sure getting back together with your wife?" he whispered. "You mentioned she was seeing someone."

The wheel spun.

"Why are you asking me this?"

"Because I think that chick has the hots for you. Every now and then, she looks this way."

The ball on the roulette wheel stopped on three. So close. "No, um....no, I love my wife. Things will work out." He stared at nothing in particular. Didn't want to draw attention to Krouse. If she was undercover, he didn't want to blow it. If she wasn't, he didn't want to cause her more trouble. Krouse was trained. She could handle it.

"She's still looking this way. Maybe it's not you she's interested in. Sorry, dude. But if you're not going for her, I'll take my chances."

"I don't think..." He pinched his lips together.

"Sir, your bet?"

Jake placed another inside bet. This time on ten. Carlotta had been born on the tenth of May. He didn't want to gamble, but he also couldn't let Randy get into trouble.

The man with sunglasses had left the table. There was something vaguely familiar about him.

Randy chose to occupy the now empty seat. The man who earlier revealed his gun still sat on the other side of Krouse. How could he get Randy out of there?

His coworker chatted with Krouse.

No, kid. Uggh. Those pickup lines never work.

Krouse averted her gaze. The man with the gun shifted in his seat and turned to face Randy, his gun now hidden from view.

Jake stood, stepped toward Randy, and shoved him.

"What are you doing, dude?" Randy asked.

"You thief!" Jake yelled. "You took all my chips! Now you're trying to steal all the ladies in this joint, too?" He grabbed Randy by the collar. A look of fear washed over his friend. After grabbing Randy, Jake tossed his coworker aside. A hand grasped Jake's shoulder. Probably the other man who had sat by Krouse. *Now what?* He spun around and struck the man in the eye. Oh, no. Detective Hadley in sunglasses. So he was undercover, too. And he'd have to maintain his cover. Hadley grabbed him and Randy by the neck and looked over at the man who had the gun.

"Show a little respect. I'm trying to play here. If there's one thing I can't stand, it's an onlooker running his mouth." He eyed Jake. "I suggest you and your friend find another table."

"My apologies." Jake grabbed Randy's arm and dragged him along. "C'mon."

Randy looked at Hadley and then at Jake. "What just happened?"

Jake avoided eye contact and kept walking.

"What just happened?" Randy repeated. "Can someone fill me in?"

"Later." He marched Randy back to his vehicle.

"Tell me what just happened?" Randy stared.

"The blonde is a friend of mine. She's a detective. The guy I hit is one, too. Apparently, they were undercover. And those were real criminals sitting next to her. And you, my friend, were about to get in between her and some bad guys. I'm sorry, but I had to think of something fast."

"That was....wow. Unbelievable." Randy grinned.

Jake sighed. Only his coworker would think almost getting hurt or taking part in an undercover sting was awesome.

~*~

On the weekend, Jake approached Rosario's apartment mid-morning and knocked. He waited several minutes. Nothing. Carlotta's car sat in the driveway. He shifted his gaze to the door. Slightly ajar. After twisting the knob, he opened the door and strode into the living room.

"Rosie?" Carlotta entered wearing a towel. Must have just stepped out of the shower. "Jake?" She tugged her towel tighter. "What are you doing here?"

"The door was unlocked and ajar. Look, can we talk?"

"About what? The lawyers are handling everything. Your attorney can send me copies of your paperwork."

"You can have whatever you want—the house, the cars, the money. Look, I came here to talk about me."

She scowled.

"That came out wrong. I've been going to a pastor for counseling. I'm changing, Carlotta. I was wondering if maybe we could put this divorce on hold. I don't want to lose you."

"You've always had a way with words. I'm sure you'll make senior editor someday. If only you meant it."

"Is it the job, baby? I could quit, and we could

move away."

"You? Quit the love of your life? Let's face it. Your job was your first affair even before the blonde."

Should he tell her Pablo saw her new friend hanging out with Allison?

"Once the paperwork is finalized, I'm no longer your wife." She turned her head away. "You can spend more time with your girlfriend."

Jake clenched his jaw. "Allison isn't my girlfriend. She was nothing more than a mistake. And now…never mind. Please, Carlotta. Please, please reconsider."

"There's nothing to reconsider, Jake. Please stop sending me flowers and notes. Please leave me alone." Carlotta motioned for him to leave.

He stopped on the doormat. Flowers and notes? "What—?"

Carlotta closed the door. Like a journalist indicating -30- at the end of a press release. End of story.

~*~

A siren blared, and a musty odor invaded Jake's nostrils as he settled into the squishy, well-worn, pea green sofa and studied the cracked plaster walls of Pablo's urban apartment. Quite a contrast from his earlier visit to Rosario's duplex. He glanced at his brother-in-law's Bible on the makeshift crate table. Jake quirked a brow. "So you're not doing drugs anymore?"

Pablo took a seat in a folding chair next to him and

smiled. "Nope. Found Jesus in prison. The real deal. Been born again."

Jake shook his head and stared at nothing in particular. "I've been to church, but I don't even know what that means."

Pablo motioned with his right hand. "So there's this rich leader, and he asks Jesus what's he gotta to do to be saved. He says unless a man is born again, he ain't gonna enter Heaven. When you accept Jesus, it's like you're born again. A new beginning."

Jake scratched his head.

Pablo pointed at Jake. "Name one thing you done wrong."

Jake chuckled. "Only one?"

"I hear ya. So we've all messed up. We deserve hell. But God sent Jesus, who was perfect, to die in our place, take our sin, so we can go to Heaven."

Jake picked up the Bible, flipped through the pages, and set it back down. "How many more good points do I need to get into Heaven?" Lying was one thing, but as far as sin levels went, he must have racked up an enormous debt.

"It's free," Pablo said. "Salvation is a free gift. You take it, and from then on, you let Jesus steer your life."

"I went to church with my grandma, and people would go to the front and kneel. I guess they were getting saved. I suppose I need to talk to this pastor I know."

"You can," said Pablo, "Or you can talk to God right now."

Jake's shoulders tightened. "Right now?"

"Yeah, why not? I mean, there's some crazy guy loose, right? Someone killed Ed." He raised both hands. "Wasn't me. But someone did, and he's out there. And what if something happens to you? Don't you wanna know where you'll go when you die?"

Jake rubbed his chin. "What do I say?"

"Ha. Ha. The newspaper man needs some words." Pablo punched Jake in the arm.

Jake grinned. "Why weren't you like this before? We could have hung out together."

"The drugs, man. Makes you do crazy things. I'm praying Rosario will take me back and let me have a life with her and Antonio."

"And if she doesn't?"

A car alarm sounded.

"Then I'll keep praying."

Faith. Pablo had it. But did he? Could he ask God to forgive him? Trust God to save him and guide him in the right direction—the same God who allowed his father to die? Nope, he wasn't ready to take that leap. Not yet. He needed more answers, more facts. And he knew where to get them.

~*~

At the animal shelter, Carlotta hooked the mixed breed dog up to a leash. The canine tugged in the opposite direction. This one would need leash training. She blew out a breath. Oh, well, there were worse ways to spend time on her day off.

She wiped sweat from her brow. Finally, the last

task for the day. The new shelter director had been teaching her how to work with the dogs. Ed had given her simple tasks, helping to clean cages, walking dogs, playing with puppies. But the new director wanted her to be more hands on with all the canines, especially the adult dogs. Her fingers trembled, and she willed them to stop. Coming back to this place since Ed's death had been hard.

Carlotta returned the dog to his cage and glanced at his nametag. She petted his muzzle. "So the name's Jake. No wonder you like control." What if Jake was serious? What if he had changed? But how could she be sure he wouldn't cheat on her again?

The mutt whimpered and tilted his head. She scratched his chin.

Jake said he'd consider more infertility treatments, but what if he changed his mind again? And he'd been adamant he didn't want a dog.

Her cell phone vibrated.

"Hello?"

"Is this Mrs. Hartman?"

She waved to the interim director as she left the building. The woman smiled and waved back. "Yes, may I ask who's speaking?"

"This is Fred's Flowers," a man with a nasally voice said. "You called and wanted to know who sent some flowers to your sister's duplex. I have the contact information. Do you want it?"

"Yes, please." Carlotta opened her car door.

"Mr. Jake Hartman sent the flowers. His address is—"

"That won't be necessary."

"Are you sure? I have his address and phone number."

"No, thank you. That won't be necessary." Carlotta ended the call. She had proof. She slumped behind the steering wheel.

Of all the sick things, and to try and tell her he'd changed. Someone was changing all right, but it wasn't him.

What had happened to Jake? Had the stress from the infertility treatments pushed him to the brink? Maybe she should have just been content without children. Could this all somehow be her fault?

~*~

At the library, Carlotta filled a paper cup with water. At least she didn't have to stress anymore about taking time off for infertility treatments. One less thing on her mind.

Someone touched her shoulder. "Girl, is everything OK? I heard you and Jake are getting a divorce," Nicole whispered.

Carlotta took a deep breath. "Wow, word travels fast." She guzzled the cool water.

"I'm sorry. I thought things were going so well. You were trying to have a baby."

"We were. Life seemed good. But it's over now. I need to move on."

"I'm so sorry. I'm here to listen if you need to talk. I was married to an alcoholic, got divorced, then remarried, and found out I'd married another addict—this time a gambler. Later, I became a Christian, and through the help of a counselor, I learned I was attracted to addicts. I had some bad habits that needed changing—something called co-dependency."

Carlotta rubbed her forehead. "I think it's too late to get Jake help."

"If you don't feel comfortable sharing with a coworker, I understand. If you'd like to speak to a counselor, let me know, and I can give you the name of mine."

"I'm not sure Jake wants to change." Would a changed man send her strange notes and flowers?

"Maybe, but it might be good for you to talk to someone."

Counseling for her? Carlotta's voice shook. "Jake cheated on me and not the other way around. You think you know someone... Dad wasn't there for me, and I thought I'd finally found someone with Jake."

"Sometimes, we're attracted to certain people, the wrong kinds, for a reason. As we go through life, we can pick up unhealthy habits from others—friends, family."

Mom was an alcoholic. Jake might have a gambling problem. Carlotta gritted her teeth. "This has nothing to do with my family." So her dad was unfaithful, too. "I know you're trying to help, but I don't need it."

Nicole's head dipped. "OK. Well, I'll be praying for you." Nicole glanced back once more before heading back to her desk. Was that a look of pity? Or disappointment that her wisdom had been rejected?

Carlotta's muscles quivered. She crumpled the paper cup and tossed it in the trash. She rushed to the bathroom and slammed the stall door behind her. Sobs racked her body as she leaned against the stall wall. After bunching up toilet paper, she used it to dry her eyes. Once she'd composed herself, she walked back to her desk, head held high.

Other people went to counseling. People with problems. People like Jake. People like Nicole and her ex-husbands.

She was fine on her own. She didn't need anyone or anything. Then why did everything hurt so much?

~*~

Jake's toes scrunched in his beige living room carpet as he paced the floor. He could change. He could go to counseling. Or take another job. Even move if need be. Whatever she wanted. They could get back together. Things could improve. He'd even try the dreaded infertility treatments again if it'd bring her back in his life.

His mind flashed to his last meeting with Carlotta. She'd closed the door not just on him, but on their relationship. So all this counseling but she might not want him to contact her again.

Jake sat on the couch, and spied his granny's Bible on the coffee table. He flipped it open—verse roulette. Song of Solomon 4:2. He read the verse. "Teeth like a flock of sheep? Huh?"

Nope, that didn't apply. A piece of paper stuck out of one end. He flipped to the bookmarked page and found a highlighted scripture passage. Probably better than his hit-and-miss method anyway. Joshua 1:9. He read the verse. Be strong, huh? Good courage? *Be not afraid. God is with thee whithersoever thou goest.*

Jake grabbed his keys and went out the door. He'd rather have her be mad at him than not warn her.

12

Carlotta pushed the book cart inside the library elevator. The faint scent of little sweaty bodies permeated the space, evidence that the children had made their way downstairs to look at books. Over the years, patrons complained about their kids doing this or that. If only they knew had badly she wanted to experience all that—having children of her own. The odor and noise weren't all bad. It meant little ones were present. *Maybe someday.*

She pressed the button for the lower level. A man in an olive-colored trench coat stepped inside the elevator cab and tipped his hat at her. It had been a little cooler today with the slight cold front associated with the rain, but not that frigid. Maybe he got chilled easily. Her grandpa always ran cold.

Uneasiness swept over her. The animal shelter break-in, the pipe bombs, the missing women... Or maybe her judgment was clouded because she'd been trapped in the elevator before with Xavier.

As the doors closed, Nicole propped her hand between them and slipped inside the cab.

Carlotta relaxed. Nicole's presence kept her from being alone in the elevator with the man. If he was some sort of bad guy, hopefully, he wouldn't try anything with someone else in the elevator.

The doors closed. Nicole pressed the button for the next floor down. The elevator moved and then stopped. A ding sounded. After the doors opened, Nicole stepped outside and turned to face Carlotta. "See you later." The doors closed, and the elevator moved again.

The cab jolted, then stopped.

Carlotta's chest tightened. The walls of the cab suddenly appeared closer.

The man stared at her. "I think it's stuck."

Carlotta nodded. She propped her back up against the cart and chewed on a nail.

Removing his hat, the man stepped closer.

Carlotta moved into the corner and used her arms to brace herself. It wasn't as if she had a weapon. Not even a pen. The emergency button was on the other wall. On the other side of the man. How would she get to it if needed? *Breathe.*

The man leaned closer. "Is everything OK?"

"Huh?" *Breathe in, breathe out.*

He stood next to her. "Are you OK? How are ya?"

"Other than being stuck inside an elevator with a stranger?"

"Sorry, let me introduce myself. I'm Tom Clyde." He stood. "Let me see here." He stood and studied the elevator button panel. He pressed the emergency call button.

A woman answered through the speaker. "Hello?"

"Hello, another patron and I are stuck in the elevator, probably somewhere between the main level and basement. Can you send some help?"

"Which elevator are you in?"

"Uh…" The man looked at Carlotta.

"Two," she answered.

"I'll have someone out to look at it shortly. Is everyone OK?"

The man gazed at Carlotta. His eyes appeared kind. Maybe she'd misjudged him.

She nodded.

"Yes, we're OK. Thank you."

The operator hung up, and the man reclined against the opposite wall of the cab.

"At least we're all OK. No medical problems, no pregnant women." He chuckled.

Carlotta huffed. No, certainly none of those.

Sudden understanding showed in the man's eyes. "I'm sorry. Did I say something or do something to offend you? You look upset."

"I… My husband and I weren't able to have children. We tried for many years, but it wasn't meant to be." Why was she even telling a stranger such things?

"I'm so sorry. I didn't know."

Yet he seemed like the kind of person who was easy to talk to. "It's OK. I'm slowly getting over it."

"My brother and his wife were infertile. They adopted three kids from China."

Last time someone got stuck in here, they didn't get out for over an hour. Stop thinking about that, concentrate on the conversation. You got this.

"That's wonderful. Unfortunately, my husband

and I aren't together anymore." Her voice came out stilted.

"I would expect infertility would put a large strain on a marriage."

She blew out a breath. The walls were closing in on her. Dreaded claustrophobia had to hit right now. "Infertility and adultery."

"Oh."

Just keep talking. Don't think about being trapped. "Yep, soon we'll be divorced."

"He didn't want to work things out?"

What was that mindfulness exercise she'd read about? "Oh, probably. But how can I trust him now? I'm sorry, this is probably too personal."

"It's OK, but if you don't want to talk about it, I understand." The man looked at his watch.

The walls were not moving. Help hadn't arrived.

Count the tiles. Maybe that would work. One. Two.

After several minutes passed, Carlotta spoke up. "Things were so difficult near the end. The divorce will make things easier."

"Hm."

"What does that mean?"

"Marriage is tough, but I don't think going through a divorce is exactly easy, either."

A loud noise. The elevator doors opened to show the heads of two workers stuck between the two floors.

"Climb out this way, please. Be careful," the man said.

"So, are you saying I should get back together

with him?" Carlotta asked as she moved to the opening.

"I'm just telling you that some wives who walk through my door don't have the opportunity for reconciliation. Some wish they did." He handed her a card and moved aside. "It was nice meeting you."

"Ma'am, this way, please." the worker beckoned.

The man gestured to the door opening. "Ladies first. Do you need some help climbing out?"

"No, thank you. I can manage." Carlotta stuffed the card in her pocket and crawled through the opening. She looked back inside the elevator cab. "My cart."

"We'll have to remove it later. I'm sorry," the worker said.

"OK. I understand. I'll be over in the nonfiction section if you need to find me later." Carlotta pointed to her nametag. "I'm Carlotta Hartman." She cringed and then walked away from the elevators. Still Hartman. Still married to Jake. Still his wife. To have and to hold, and all that other stuff. She shook her head. No, he'd thrown that all away with his affair. He didn't want her anymore. Maybe he and the blonde would get married and have children, have the happy family the two of them never could have. She pulled the man's card from her pocket and examined it. Thomas Clyde, Senior Pastor, Cincinnati Evangelical Free Church. Hadn't she and Jake visited there once or twice several years ago? Minus the hat and trench coat, he seemed familiar.

She stuffed the card back in her pocket and strode

over to the newspapers. Hopefully, the workers would have her cart freed soon, and she could get back to work. She spread a newspaper across a table and sat down. She studied the latest editorial on the missing women. Where were they being taken? What happened to them? Carlotta pinched the skin at her throat. Could this somehow be related to the break-in at the animal shelter, or were they unrelated? What if she had been at the animal shelter that night instead of Ed? She could be missing, too, or worse. She squeezed her eyes shut. A firm hand grasped her shoulder. Her eyes shot open, and she gasped.

Geoffrey stood behind her.

Carlotta relaxed. "Whew. It's only you." She pointed to the paper. "Have you read about the missing women?"

Geoffrey nodded. "It is tragic." He took a seat next to her. "What is the matter?"

"What if that night at the animal shelter, someone was trying to kidnap me?"

"Then I would have heard you scream and would have come running to your rescue."

Carlotta turned back toward the newspaper article. "I'm serious, Geoffrey."

"What if the break-in had nothing to do with you? For all you know, someone was targeting the man who worked there."

She put a hand to her chin. "You really think so?"

"I do. And I do not think you should spend any more time worrying about it."

Carlotta nodded.

"I have to run to the market across the street, but I hope you will still meet me for dinner later." He smiled.

"Sounds good. But I'm paying for my meal."

Geoffrey left.

Carlotta smoothed the newspaper and then opened it again and scanned the photos of the missing women. Younger than her, but all brunettes. Just like her. She held her stomach and bent forward. Geoffrey said things would be OK. Now if only she could convince her digestive tract.

~*~

Jake watched the nightly news. Three women missing so far. He clicked off the TV. His gaze shifted to the opposite side of the room and settled on a well-worn recliner. Now empty. His chest ached. Jake stumbled to the chair and touched the neatly folded red, black, and white college team throw draped over it. After rubbing his fingers along the edge, he brought it closer to his nose and inhaled the scent of Carlotta's floral perfume. What if someone kidnapped Carlotta? Or Kelsey? Or even Rosario. Though he and his sister-in-law didn't always get along, he wished her no harm. Bottom line—someone was out there taking these women.

He picked up his phone and dialed a number. "Randy, are you busy tonight?"

"Are you hitting on me, Jake?" Randy chuckled. "Sorry, dude. After the whole thing with Allison." He snorted and his voice took a more serious tone.

"What did you have in mind?"

"I want to meet and discuss what you've found so far on Geoffrey Walters."

Gracie scurried toward him.

"Sure. I mean, not much so far. Just one question for you though. Is this about your wife, or do you really think it pertains to the triad?"

Gracie pounced on him.

"A valid question. And to be honest, a bit of both."

"Your wife? So you really aren't into Allison?"

Jake scratched the kitten's head. "I made a mistake. I love my wife. I want to get her back."

"That's deep, dude." Randy nodded. "Almost as deep as I feel about Super Techie Girl. A total babe. Did I tell you what she did in the latest episode of *Nerd World*?"

"You didn't." *But I guess I'll hear about it, anyway.* "Why don't you swing by my place. I'll order pizza, and we can discuss the details."

"Sounds good. Make sure you order anchovies."

Jake flinched. Anchovies? He'd better warn Randy not to mention that to Stu, at least if he ever wanted to move up the ladder in the newspaper world.

Gracie purred. She would probably like some anchovies.

Several minutes later, the doorbell rang. Could Randy be here already? Jake hurried to the front door and opened it. "Carlotta?"

The rookie journalist returned his stare. "Sorry, dude. Only me, Randy. Hey, is that jazz music?"

"You like it?"

Randy nodded. "I come bearing good news. Well, maybe not good, but at least juicy."

Jake quirked a brow. Hopefully not about Allison and him.

Holding Gracie in one hand, Jake motioned for Randy to come inside.

The scent of incense followed Randy. Jake's eyes widened, and his mouth opened. Jake could remind the kid of Stu's rules regarding incense another day. They had far more important matters to discuss.

Jake set Gracie on the floor, and she scampered into another room.

Then he relaxed on the recliner while Randy sat on the couch.

His coworker read from a notepad. "Jake, I think you need to hear this. I found some stuff on the lawyer. I don't know how to say this, but...this dude could be our psychopath. I used the information I found on him to locate people close to him. Then I followed up with interviews with any willing participants."

"What did you tell them?"

"That I worked for the newspaper. I was careful. I flashed a press badge. I didn't indicate which paper, and none of them asked."

"And what did you find?" Ugh. He'd forgotten to check up on the jogger from Eden Park to see if he'd reported on her before. Maybe he could remember to do that the next time he was in the office.

Randy studied his notepad. "Two people. Neither wanted to go on record. A dude and a chick who went to high school with him. They described him as disturbed." His coworker emphasized the last word using air quotes. "They said his family moved into the area when he was in high school. He was a loner, kept to himself most of the time. Dude didn't appear to like school much, except for a biology class, where they dissected animals. This seemed to excite him. During his senior year, several pets in town went missing. Then the year after he left for college, the disappearances stopped."

A chill swept down Jake's spine. "Did anyone report any suspicions they might have had about him?"

"They were too afraid. Apparently, Geoffrey Walters, aka Allen Jeffery Barr, lived with his grandma, but during his senior year, the two of them argued, and she died. The official ruling: death by natural causes. But the two classmates said some townsfolk had their suspicions."

"Moved in with Grandma? And moved again at least once while living with her. I wonder what his life was like before that."

"While some believe genetics influences psychopathy more than upbringing, at least one well-known study has shown many psychopaths had unstable home lives. So maybe nurture is involved in addition to nature."

Jake rubbed his neck. "Hmm."

"Walters attended college for two years, studying biology but dropped out after a lab tech accused him of trying to steal a cadaver. Then he dropped out of school and supposedly moved away. Walters then enrolled at another university two hundred miles away and got his history degree. He then attended law school. During this time, several animals died mysteriously or went missing. One person talked about how bad they felt for him because his pets always died, said he was such an unlucky dude."

Bile rose from Jake's throat. "An unlucky man or pure evil. We've got our suspicions. Do I go to the police now?"

Randy leaned closer. "That was the thing. I wondered why no one went before. They all seemed scared. That and they said he was very convincing. Like the dude was totally influential. Does he have any friends at the Cincinnati Police Department? I'm not talking dirty cops, but anyone he might have influence over, like maybe in the way of blackmail?"

Maybe that's why he'd been at the courthouse the other day. Or maybe he was working on a case. After all, he was a lawyer. Jake rubbed the back of his neck. "I'll need to find out." He could trust Detective Krouse, but should he include her, tell her what he knew? If Walters/Barr was as evil and powerful as he seemed, talking to Krouse could be risky for both of them.

"You mean we." Randy pointed at himself and then at Jake, "You can't do this alone."

"You've already done enough. I want you to sit this out. This guy is crazy. I don't want him to have any reason to come near you."

"Hey, dude." Randy shook his head. "No one is coming after the Rand-man. And if he does, I'll taze him, bro."

He spoke big, but if Walters had killed before… "Be careful."

The doorbell rang again.

Randy quirked a brow. His pupils dilated. "Expecting someone?"

Jake chuckled. "Relax. It's only the pizza guy." He got his wallet and opened the door. "Hi."

The delivery guy gave him the pizza and then rattled off the total.

After removing several bills, Jake handed them to the man. "Keep the change."

The man pocketed the cash. "Thanks."

Jake put the pizza on the coffee table. "I'll get some plates." He brought back paper plates, napkins, and sodas and set them by the opened pizza box.

Jake opened a soda and released a breath he didn't realize he'd been holding.

"What's the matter, dude?"

Jake took a bite of pizza. Sauce dribbled on his chin. He grabbed a napkin to wipe it. "I don't know. I feel as if I should know this Allen Jeffery Barr from somewhere, but I can't figure out why I would know him." His mind raced through thousands of articles he'd written, events he'd covered, lives on which he'd reported.

"He's invading your psyche. What I call *Linda Vu*."

"Déjà vu?"

His coworker took a bite of pizza and then shook his head. "No, Linda. She was this gamer I met online. That chick tried to implant herself in my thoughts. Like in that movie. A dream within a dream within a…creep-y."

"Hey, Randy."

Randy stared at him. "Yeah, man."

"Never tell Stu about Linda Vu, OK?" Jake laughed.

Randy gave him a thumbs up. "Got it. Mention Vu to Stu, and I'm in deep doo doo."

Jake sighed. On a mission to stop a killer with Randy as his sidekick. What could go wrong? More like, what could go right?

13

Carlotta hurried toward the ball park to find Geoffrey. She jogged up the stairs and then gazed around the outdoor private box. Heat crept up her face. She tugged on her white denim shorts. Sure, she'd lost a little weight since she stopped taking the fertility hormones, but this pair didn't suit her. Too short for her taste, but Rosario thought they were just right. They might have come from the same family, had the same parents, but their tastes weren't always the same.

Geoffrey ambled toward her and grabbed her hand. "Thank you for coming."

"Thank you for inviting me."

He handed her a baseball hat.

"Thanks." She put it on, noting Geoffrey did too.

They took in a few innings and then sampled the food.

When they returned to their seats, a newcomer joined them. Geoffrey gestured toward the man. "I would like you to meet Bernard Leonard. He is an associate. Bernard, I would like to introduce you to a friend, Carlotta Hartman."

"Nice to meet you," Bernard said. "Hartman? No relation to that newspaper journalist?"

Geoffrey placed his hand on Carlotta's shoulder.

"None whatsoever."

Carlotta arched a brow.

Bernard excused himself.

Leaning closer, Geoffrey whispered to her. "Do not worry. You will soon be free of any association with Jake Hartman."

Carlotta slumped.

Geoffrey tilted his head. "What is it? What did Mr. Hartman do?"

"I think he's been talking to my brother-in-law, Pablo. Pablo says he saw you with another woman, the same one Jake had an affair with. Not that it's any of my concern that you did. She just doesn't seem like the type of person you would be friends with." Geoffrey could date whoever he wanted. Although, it would feel like a conflict of interest with the divorce proceedings if he were to date Blondie.

"Hmmm...I am not sure what he thought he saw, but obviously, he was wrong."

"I figured as much. I don't know what's gotten into Jake. Drugs made my brother-in-law act differently. I wonder if..."

He grabbed her hand. "While I do not want to appear to take Jake's side, keep in mind you heard this from your brother-in-law. You just mentioned he's an addict..."

"Former addict."

Geoffrey raised a brow. "I do believe people can change. However, it has been my personal experience that addicts often fall back in old patterns. Promise me you and your sister will be on your guard around him."

Geoffrey was kind. Maybe too much so. Trying to put the blame on Pablo and not Jake. "I will. I'm sorry I even brought it up. You're right. As always."

The hot dogs, the game, the view—the only way it could have been better was if Jake had been there, as he had earlier in their marriage. Too bad her trips with him to ballgames in the past had often been connected to work, his first love.

"Is everything OK?" Geoffrey asked.

Carlotta smiled. "Yes."

A camera panned around the ball park. Carlotta looked at the screen. An elderly couple kissed. Then a young couple. Who would be next?

Geoffrey leaned toward her and whispered, "I wonder if the home team will win."

She glanced at the screen. Oh, no. It had captured Geoffrey leaning toward her. They hadn't kissed, but what would Jake think?

Warmth radiated through her body and not just from the August sun. Carlotta did her best to tug her baseball cap down even more.

Jake would be sure to see this. Who wouldn't? Right there in front of God and everyone. She fidgeted with the cross necklace. God. What did He think about all this? Jake had sure been mentioning God a lot lately.

So did Dad. He'd cheat on Mom but was sure to attend church and act pious during the service. So did Mom. She'd get drunk but often still attended.

One thing about her new friend Geoffrey. No one

could accuse him of being a hypocrite. He didn't adhere to a religion, or at least not one he'd shared with Carlotta.

Geoffrey smiled at her. A look that conveyed complete acceptance.

~*~

Jake drove to Rosario's duplex to confront Carlotta. Rosario's car wasn't in the driveway. A good sign. At least he wouldn't have to deal with two angry women. Plus, Carlotta might listen to him more if Rosario wasn't around to poison her mind, which was one reason he hadn't cared much for his sister-in-law. He knocked on the door.

Carlotta opened it, glanced at him, and started to shut it.

Jake wedged his arm in the doorway. "This Geoffrey guy, what do you know about him, Carlotta? I mean *really* know about him."

Stepping back from the door, she raised her voice. "What do you mean? I suppose you don't like him."

"I still care about you. And, you're right, I don't like him. I think he's dangerous."

Carlotta rolled her eyes. "Because he was there that night at the animal shelter? Look, the police questioned him, Jake. One of his coworkers vouched for him. So he has a solid alibi."

Jake shrugged. "Maybe they lied."

"What? Do you hear yourself, Jake? Why would a coworker, especially a lawyer, someone familiar with the ramifications of the law, lie to cover up a murder?"

"He wouldn't happen to have plastic bed sheets, by chance?"

Carlotta's face turned red. "How would I? Even if…"

"While it's not been studied extensively, there's a hypothesis that says there may be three characteristics of a psychopath, killing animals, fire-starting, and bedwetting. Look, Carlotta, please stay away from him. I don't want you to get hurt. I don't want to read about you in the paper. I don't want you to end up like Ed or that jogger who was almost kidnapped. Or those missing women."

"You know," Carlotta said, "I read that the suspect in the jogger case was barefoot. Same for the animal shelter suspect."

He narrowed his gaze. Why hadn't he heard this before? This information must have come in after the initial police report. He'd have to talk to Detective Krouse the next time he got the chance. Wait. Was that why Kelsey had asked about his whereabouts that night? He had a solid alibi. Had interviewed the mayor and had been at work. A dozen witnesses could vouch for him. Well, almost. Count out Allison.

"That's right. Barefoot. That pretty much describes half your family, Jake. You want to talk about alibis. Where was your uncle both nights? The man's constantly chasing down conspiracy theories. For all we know, he might have killed, thinking the government was after him. And you used to jog by that park a lot."

Right on all accounts. Where was she going with this? "You think *I* had something to do with the attempted kidnapping of the jogger?"

"No, but you are pointing a finger at Geoffrey when someone could do the same to you or your uncle."

Jake cracked his knuckles. "This is not about my uncle. This is about keeping you safe. I read enough depressing news. I don't care to read any more dark headlines or to see any gruesome photos, especially not about people I care about." His voice grew husky. "People I love."

"Gruesome photos?" Carlotta tilted her head.

"The picture from the baseball game. You and that guy up on the big screen." That thug's mouth touching his wife. Ew. Some seriously ugly thoughts toward the guy ran through his mind. And this was only a kiss. Carlotta had every right to be upset about his affair. If Geoffrey and Carlotta had slept together... He clenched his fists, couldn't let his mind go there.

"Jake, it's not how it looks. It was so loud. He was just leaning over to talk to me."

He blew out a breath. "Carlotta, I'm an idiot. I admit it. But please don't ruin your life over me."

"Jake, you're the one who had the affair. You're the one who has been sending crazy notes and flowers. I'm worried about you. This isn't like you."

"I didn't send you anything." Though maybe he should send her some flowers, chocolates, or something nice.

Carlotta folded her arms. "That's not what the

florist said."

He raised his voice. "Well, they're wrong."

"Why would the florist lie to me, Jake?"

He shrugged. "I don't know. Maybe someone impersonated me or paid the florist to lie."

"Really? A conspiracy theory? You sound like your uncle. This is not like you."

"I needed to talk to you, to warn you."

"Jake, I think you might need some help. A counselor, maybe."

"Carlotta. Please be careful. Get to know this guy more. Don't blow this off simply to get even with me. I fear for your safety. I have a friend from work who looked into Geoffrey's past."

She blinked rapidly. "You did what?"

"Geoffrey's a complete psychopath. We need to contact the police."

Carlotta rubbed an eyebrow. "So why haven't you?"

"Honestly, I've been concerned he might have some police connections—dirty cops."

"So why bother contacting them now?"

"I know at least one officer I can trust. This can't wait any longer. I need to tell her."

She let out a slight growl. "Her? Oh, I bet you know her."

"He starts small, Carlotta…killing animals. Then he moves on to the perfect victim. That's you."

Her left eye twitched. She moved toward the coffee machine and turned it on. "A victim? The only one who's been sending me threatening letters is you."

"It wasn't me."

Carlotta deepened her tone. "But the florist gave me your name. There's proof."

"Anyone could have sent flowers and given my name."

Carlotta shook her head. "So you're saying Geoffrey killed the dogs at the shelter? And Ed? What about him? That would mean Geoffrey already killed, which would ruin your convoluted theory."

"I heard recently that Ed's official cause of death was a heart attack. Maybe Ed simply died of fright."

"Or you could be confused. Like your uncle. Sometimes those things are hereditary."

"I'm not paranoid."

"Honestly, Jake. From my viewpoint, that's not how it looks. Rosario suggested I get a restraining order. I don't want to do that, Jake." She lowered her voice, "Just please leave me alone."

~*~

As Carlotta put away books, a novel cover caught her eye. *Catcher in the Rye*. She hadn't seen Xavier or heard from the police about him. Didn't he live near the florist shop? He'd mentioned the name of his apartment building once. Could he have sent the notes?

As she entered her boss's office, Carlotta studied the modern art reproduction on the wall—orange and white paint strategically drizzled onto a canvas. Becca was quite the Jackson Pollock fan. Carlotta glanced at her watch. Five minutes past the original meeting time and ten minutes until her work day ended.

Becca stumbled inside—her blue suit remained pressed, but her hairdo was disheveled. "Sorry, I'm late." She plopped books on her desk and inhaled a deep breath. After fixing her hair, she took a seat across from Carlotta. "I won't keep you long. I don't have the recent budget, but the supervisors have been discussing it. There are a lot of cuts coming. We might eliminate positions. I wanted to let you know. You're already going through a lot right now."

Carlotta let out a breath. Yes, she was. First a divorce and maybe losing a job now, too?

Becca leaned closer and met Carlotta's gaze. "You're an exceptional librarian. You've been here for a while, so I assume you should be safe. But you never know in this economy. So if you decide to look elsewhere, I'd be glad to write you a letter of recommendation."

Carlotta removed a small fuzz from her blouse. "When will you find out?"

Becca faced her computer and typed notes. "The new budget won't be approved right away. Maybe three more months?"

Again, Carlotta glanced at her watch. "How definite is this?"

Becca faced Carlotta and folded her hands. "It sounds pretty set in stone. I don't know how many positions will be eliminated, but at least some."

"Thank you." Carlotta left Becca's office and finished a few remaining tasks. She stood. Time to meet Geoffrey for dinner. She went home to get ready.

~*~

Carlotta came out of her bedroom wearing a new blouse and jeans.

Rosario gave her a once over. "Where are you off to?"

"Geoffrey and I are going out to dinner."

Rosario nodded and returned her attention to Antonio.

Carlotta drove to the restaurant, trying not to think of anything at all.

Geoffrey was already seated and had ordered a drink.

A waitress approached the table.

"I'd like a diet soda," Carlotta said. "Oh, and we'd like separate checks, please."

The waitress nodded and hurried away.

"Why the long face?" He raised a brow. "Did Mr. Hartman do something?"

Carlotta shook her head. "No, just work-related stuff."

"Do you want to talk about it?"

"Becca, my boss, mentioned budget cuts, positions being eliminated. It might not even happen, but she wanted to give me a heads up. If my sister gets back together with Pablo, I'll become a third wheel."

"You know, if you are tired of living with your sister, my secretary might have an extra room. I will ask her the next time I see her."

After dinner, Carlotta and Geoffrey sauntered outside.

Carlotta squinted as they neared her car. "Not another one!"

"What is it?"

She snatched a note from her car and tore it in two.

"What did it say?"

"It doesn't matter." She dropped the pieces of the note. "Good-bye. I'm going home now."

Geoffrey leaned closer and blinked. "Are you sure? Do you want me to follow your car home? Will you be OK?"

She swallowed hard. "I'll be fine." She waved to Geoffrey from inside her car, and then started the vehicle. Her hands trembled as she touched the steering wheel.

She drove down the street and took quick peeks into the backseat. No one was there. "I'm OK. Everything is OK." She flicked on the overhead light.

When she got to Rosario's place, the main rooms were empty. Her sister and nephew must have gone to bed already.

Carlotta entered the kitchen. Her Christmas cactus set next to the window, leaves badly burnt. Poor Elizabeth. Jake had warned about too much sunlight. Probably needed more water. The pitiful thing didn't have much fight in it. Sort of like her at this moment.

14

After his morning walk on the treadmill, Jake got some water.

"Meow."

He looked at Gracie. "Are you hungry?" He picked up the kitten and scratched beneath her tiny chin. She produced a purr.

Jake walked over to her bowl. "Almost empty." He shook the plastic container of kitten kibble. Only a few pieces remained inside. "Uh-oh. I better go to the store."

As he drove to the grocery store, he turned on the radio. Jazz music played. Nope. Not in the mood. Too somber. He switched to a country station. His and Carlotta's song played. The one about the couple. How they were still together through everything. He turned it up and sang along. His eyes misted.

Jake went inside the grocery store, still troubled. As he paid for the food at the self-checkout, his stomach rumbled. He trekked back to his car and stuffed the cat food in the trunk.

Several lunch trucks were parked nearby. Mmm...the scent of Mexican food drifted toward him. Couldn't be as good as Carlotta's cooking, but he'd settle for today.

He ordered and then paid for his food. After getting his tacos, he walked back to his car. Mmm. It smelled so good. He could hardly wait. He glanced at the food truck again. If the food tasted as good as it looked and smelled, he might need to come here again. He returned home and fed Gracie. She curled up on the carpet and drifted asleep. Jake opened his lunch and savored the rich flavor of the chicken tacos and pico de gallo. He'd definitely get food from there again. Could he feature them in the food section?

He settled onto the couch and flicked on the TV. As he lay there, a rumbling sounded from his stomach. Uh-oh. He hurried to the bathroom. Minutes later, he returned to the living room and rubbed his stomach. Good food. But Carlotta's cooking was superior. Still spicy and tasty, but it never made him sick.

Jake scrolled through his files to find their last picture together. He came across the photo of Tonya Miller and her friends. None of the three women had been found yet. All three had gone to parties and…

His eyes widened. He dialed a number. "Detective Krouse, please."

"Hello, Krouse speaking."

He tapped his foot. "Kelsey, it's Jake."

"I can't tell you—"

He pinched the bridge of his nose and squeezed his eyes tight. "I don't need anything. But I might have some information for you. The women who were missing. The college students. I tried to interview Brittany Stone's family, but they asked me to leave."

A sigh came through the speaker.

He paced the room. "Wait. The sister let it slip that she'd attended the party, too. Didn't want her mom and dad or the police to know because she's underage and had been drinking. She mentioned tacos."

"Tacos? I don't see how that's important."

He clenched his jaw. "Tonya Miller played basketball."

"Yes, Jake. I appreciate it, but I've spoken to—"

"Wait, another player mentioned eating spicy food and getting sick. Today, I had tacos from this food truck in town, and I wondered. Who catered each event?"

"I—I don't know. Interesting angle. Thank you."

"You're welcome. I hope you find whoever took those students."

Jake sank back onto the couch. He wasn't much for prayer, but he'd definitely try to think good thoughts. Krouse was the one who prayed. Hopefully, God would hear and answer her request.

~*~

Jake settled into his office chair. After work, he and Randy could go to Detective Krouse with the information Randy had collected. They could discuss it over dinner—pizza at Randy's place, sans anchovies for his pizza—so he could meet and make a copy of everything Randy had found. As Randy had said, it was good insurance, making sure more than one of them had proof.

Stu interrupted his thoughts. "I need to see you in

my office, pronto."

"What's up?" Jake asked. "Am I off probation? Can we finally get back to business as usual? It's about time."

His boss sighed dejectedly. "You're an outstanding employee. I hate to do this, Jake."

"Hate to do what?" Jake's thoughts grew fuzzy.

Stu cleared his throat and avoided Jake's gaze.

Leaning closer, Jake lowered his voice. "You're firing me? I didn't do anything." Why was so much of that night with Allison a blur? Repressed memories?

Stu clasped his hands together. "Buddy, I believe you, but Allison has created quite a stink. The company doesn't want things to look bad."

Jake let out a laugh with an edge. "So I lose my job over this? A job I have invested years into?"

"Look, I know the senior editor of a newspaper in Dayton. Maybe I can see if he can hire you."

"When am I canned, officially?" Jake asked.

"Effective immediately." Stu glanced at his watch and then propped a cheek on his fist. "Security should be here any minute to walk you out."

"Where's Randy? I need to talk to him."

"I haven't seen him. Hasn't come in yet."

Jake marched to Randy's desk. Not there. He walked over to Ann's desk. She had to have seen him around. "Where's Randy?"

"He isn't in yet." Ann emphasized each syllable and then looked away as if he were infectious. Ugh. Allison had gotten to all his coworkers.

Someone tugged his shoulder. Jake turned around

to face a security guard. "Sir, I'm here to walk you out. If you have any personal belongings left behind, someone will mail them to you." The kid couldn't have been older than twenty-five, skinny, and pimple-faced. Not much more than a mall cop. What would he do if Jake made a scene? Jake huffed and followed his escort through the maze of desks. They took the elevator down to the first floor. Then Jake exited the building and went to his car. He took one last look at his former workplace and groaned.

Randy and the only copy of proof—probably like his job—were no longer in existence.

~*~

Jake tossed his keys on the kitchen counter and huffed. Geoffrey must have gotten to Randy. No other explanation.

Gracie meowed, and he bent down to pet her.

Animal cruelty. One characteristic of a psychopath. His jaw clenched. Who could harm helpless little animals, and humans, too?

Once Jake sat down on the couch, he flicked on the television. He watched fifteen minutes of a sitcom and then clenched his fists and stood.

I can't just sit here and do nothing. He had to find out what happened. Jake stomped into the kitchen and grabbed the keys.

After two wrong turns, he ended up at Randy's apartment, hurried up to Randy's porch, and scanned the area. No one else in sight. Jake removed a credit card from his wallet. It was worth a try. He slipped it in the doorframe and slid the card up and down. Bam. The door opened. Too easily almost. As if someone had already tampered with the lock.

Jake gasped. Would he find Randy's body inside? "Randy?"

Jake inched into the living room. Everything was in order. Well, in order by Randy's standards. Stale pizza filled the air. But no signs of ransacking. Jake checked the other rooms. No signs of Randy.

How odd. A fire safe on Randy's bed, and next to it, a passport with the name Allen Jeffery Barr. Jake picked up the documents and froze. Why did it contain a photo of Randy? His hands shook. Newspaper clippings of the attempted kidnapping of the jogger in Eden Park, the break-in at the animal shelter, the disappearances of three women in town. APCC membership materials. No, this couldn't be right. Something didn't fit. Yet there it was in front of him. Had he worked with a psychopath all along? Was Randy working with Xavier, the guy from the library? Xavier had an alibi, but what if Randy didn't? No, Randy was with him that night. His insides churned. Except for when he interviewed the mayor, right before then.

A truck engine drew Jake to the window. A package van rolled up the street. Jake moved to the front door and locked it. He'd have to slip out the back. Jake waited until the package van stopped next door before he exited out the back door, careful to relock the door behind him.

He got back in his car and gazed at his hands. He'd forgotten to wipe his fingerprints off the knob, plus, he'd touched the passport. Would Randy realize he'd been there? No time to think. Randy might be back at any time now.

Starting his car in a hurry, he took care not to exit the apartment complex too quickly.

About a mile away, he pulled to the side of the road and parked to collect his thoughts. So he'd been wrong about Geoffrey? Carlotta wasn't friends with a madman after all. Jake put his hand to his head. His temple pounded. Nothing made sense at the moment.

15

The following day, Jake went to the dimly lit hamburger joint and took a seat in the red booth. He grabbed a menu from the table and motioned for Pastor Clyde to sit across from him. "Thank you for meeting with me." He rubbed his chin. Jake needed to talk to Detective Krouse about what he'd just uncovered, but he hadn't wanted to cancel his appointment with the pastor. This wasn't a conversation to do over the phone or text. As much as he didn't care for Geoffrey, at least the guy would probably keep an eye on Carlotta for now.

Pastor Clyde studied a menu. "You're welcome. I haven't heard from you in a while. How have you been?"

"I saw my brother-in-law recently."

A server approached the table. She had a pencil stashed behind a mess of short blonde curls. "What can I get you to drink?"

Jake gestured to Pastor Clyde.

"I'll have a soda."

"The same. And I think we're ready to order, too. I'll have the garbage burger with everything on it. And onion rings."

"Sounds good to me. I'll have the same."

The server strolled away.

Pastor Clyde crossed his arms. "So you were saying about your brother-in-law…"

"The guy used to be quite a wreck, strung out on drugs. Mean, nasty. I saw him recently. He'd completely changed. Said he got saved. I've read stories of criminals who say they found God for parole purposes, but I kind of think, for Pablo, it's real. Like His faith in God has changed him. So, frankly, I'm interested." Jake gazed at the pastor with sudden focus.

The server returned and set their colas on the table.

Pastor Clyde took a sip from his glass. "I sense a hesitation."

"If God exists, doesn't seem like He cares much about little kids. At least He didn't seem to care enough to save my dad."

"From your perspective, it sure would seem that way, right? But God loved you so much He sent His Son to die for you."

Jake nodded. Yep, he'd heard it before. He wasn't sure how much stock he put into it.

"Sounds as if you want to know why bad things happen?"

"Yep."

"God made everything perfect, but people sinned. Death became a part of life. Sin doesn't affect just us, but the Earth, too." He paused. "But death isn't the end. If someone is saved, they can spend eternity in Heaven."

"What about my dad? What if he's not there? I was a kid. I don't know what he believed."

"You don't know your dad didn't get saved before he died. And if he didn't, do you think he'd want you to go to Heaven?"

Jake nodded.

The waitress returned with two plates of food. "Careful, boys, it's hot."

Not as scorching and fiery as hell. That'd be steamier. "Why does a loving God send people to hell?"

"Everyone has a choice. God doesn't force people to accept Him. Adam and Eve had a choice. So did your dad. You have a choice. Choose to spend eternity with God or choose to spend it apart from Him."

Jake finished a bite of his burger. "What about people in jungles who've never heard about God?"

"God's made himself known. I've heard of people in remote places having dreams from God. He can reach people in many ways... I know you mentioned your affair. Maybe God will use that."

"How? I've lost my wife, my job." He lowered his gaze and bit his lip. "I might have a problem with gambling." He took another bite of the burger.

The pastor nodded understandably. "Now, all you have to depend on is God."

Pastor Clyde said it as if that was a good thing. The man answered his questions though, gave him a lot to ponder. "What if I can't do this?"

"You can with God's help. He gives us strength."

"Like extra muscles?"

The pastor chuckled. "Not exactly. If someone accepts Jesus as their Savior and allows Him to control their life, then they have the power of the Holy Spirit living in them."

"The Holy Spirit?" Jake bit back a smirk.

"Sound good?"

He tapped his fingers on the table. "A bit twelve-stepish. That whole Higher Power in the clouds stuff. But not bad. Good actually. How does someone let a God they can't see run their life?"

"They read the Bible and do what it says, not what they want to do. The Bible should guide believers, not society or even feelings." Pastor Clyde's phone buzzed. He looked down at it for a moment and stood. He laid some cash on the table. "Here, I'm sorry. I have to go. There's been an accident, and I have to meet a family at the hospital. Take this." Pastor Clyde handed him a Gospel tract and shook his head. "A drunk driver tried to make a U-turn and hit a family. One family member has died; the others are seriously injured. You don't have to decide this minute, Jake, but you also don't want to put it off forever."

Jake waved at Pastor Clyde and then sent Detective Krouse a text about meeting to discuss Randy's disappearance. He finished his burger and onion rings, paid the server, and took the tract to his car. He opened it and then closed it. Life wasn't that short. He could look at it later. Besides, considering all the things he'd done, would God want to take a chance on someone like him?

~*~

After dinner that evening, Jake eyed the medical bill in his hand. Charge after charge for infertility treatments. Bills stacking up. Plus, the car towing charge. Kitty food. Kitty litter. Vet bills. He bit his lip. He checked his phone. No messages from Krouse. He'd called her after his meeting with the pastor, but she wasn't in right now. Probably on another undercover assignment.

He could have called and warned Carlotta, but considering she thought he was crazy, it wasn't a good idea.

Emptiness hovered over him the way Stu would often stand behind him while he edited his final drafts. He spied the photo of Granny on the fireplace, grabbed it, and flipped it face down. Even the whiskey didn't satisfy this evening. What was missing from his life? Gambling, maybe? His wife wasn't coming back. No reason to curb his habit.

A twinge of something—guilt maybe—washed over him. Was there more to life than all this? Had the pastor been right? He huffed. A Holy Spirit helping him? He could use some help right about now.

Jake grabbed his keys and drove toward Kentucky, toward the river. He parked in the casino lot and headed inside to the slots. The stench of alcohol and smoke drifted throughout. *What am I doing here? Maybe I should call Pastor Clyde. Then again, why should he waste his time on someone like me? I'm a lost cause.*

After getting a bucket of change, he plunked

himself down on a stool in front of a machine. He pulled the lever, and the slots spun around. Cherry and two lemons. Try again. Lemon, cherry, cherry. Again. And again. He eyed the empty bucket. Like his life. Very empty right now. His mind drifted to the bills that arrived earlier. Then he eyed the empty bucket. A lot a good gambling had done. Jake set down the bucket and headed for the door.

Jake.

He glanced around the parking lot. No one right near him. He shook his head. *Great, now I'm hearing things.* Jake put the keys in the ignition but didn't start the vehicle. He glanced at the passenger seat that held the tract from Pastor Clyde. He opened it and read a few words. *I'm not sure I can do this right now. Maybe when I get home.* He stuffed it in his pocket.

Jake started the car and headed down the street. He drove for several blocks before he entered the interstate. After he cruised along for a mile, his phone dinged. What if Carlotta had sent a text? He grabbed his phone. Spam message.

As he looked up, adrenaline raced through his body. The cars in front of him had stopped, only his was still moving. He slammed on the brakes. His car swerved around other cars but still fishtailed and sideswiped the guardrail. His vehicle whipped around so now he faced oncoming traffic.

A tractor trailer a bit of distance away honked its horn and put on its brakes.

This was it. There was no way out of this. Please, God, help me.

The truck tires screeched a haunting, ungodly sound—the kind that sticks with someone for life. Lurching forward, the truck connected with his vehicle.

Pow. Whoosh. The airbag deployed.

Jake paused for a moment. What just happened? His hands shook. He'd been hit, but not too hard. He was still alive. After willing his hands to stop shaking, Jake glanced at the other driver. The man appeared to be OK, too.

Minutes later, sirens broke the silence.

An officer approached the vehicle. The man's voice, and everything else seemed suddenly louder.

Jake lowered the window.

"Are you OK?" the officer asked.

His limbs shook. "Yes, sir. But I'll need a tow truck."

"The paramedics are here. You should let them check you out. Make sure you didn't injure anything."

Did pride count? "Thank you."

The officer went to speak to the truck driver, and Jake stepped out of the vehicle. The officer set up cones around the vehicles to help direct traffic away from the area.

Jake approached the ambulance. Minutes later, after he received a clean bill of health, the tow driver arrived. *That was fast.* Must have been listening to the police scanner. He approached the driver. "Can you give me a ride to a car rental agency?"

"Sorry. No can do. I can drop you off at the gas station at the corner. It's on my way."

"Never mind. Drop the car off at my house. Here's the address. I'll just call someone else." Like who? Not his estranged wife or her sister. Not his ex-boss. Not Allison. Randy had gone missing. The pastor was probably busy. He wiped sweat from his brow. Not a single person he could count on.

Jake. You can count on Me.

He'd prayed, hadn't he? And God protected Him. Was it God?

He pulled up an app on his phone and scheduled a ride.

Cars whizzed by on the side of the road as he crossed to the shoulder. Where was that ride? *That was it. He'd schedule another one. No! Uh-uh. Not a black screen.* He scanned the horizon. Several feet away was the gas station. Maybe he could get help there. He stuffed his dead phone in his pocket.

"Honk." A car sped down the ramp and about knocked him over. *Jerk.*

As he approached the gas station, something wasn't quite right. Why was there scaffolding everywhere? He studied the sign out front. *Closed for repairs. What?*

Another sign caught his attention. He took a deep breath. OK, there was another station. Half a mile up the road. No big deal. He crossed the street and staggered to the other one.

A chime rang as he entered the establishment. He stepped in line behind four other customers. What was taking so long? How many lotto scratchers could someone need? Finally, his turn. "Can I use your phone?"

"Sorry," a young male clerk said.

"You don't understand. My car broke down. I called for a ride but no one came. My cell phone died."

The clerk shrugged. "I'm sorry. Still can't use the phone."

Jake muttered through clenched teeth. "Then how about the restroom."

The clerk didn't look up. "For paying customers only."

Grabbing a pack of gum, Jake slammed it on the counter.

The clerk rang it up and handed him the bathroom key.

After using the restroom, Jake trudged outside, leaning against the outside of the building. Two rats scurried by. The bathroom was filthy, smelly, disgusting, unclean. Which was how his life felt. He rubbed his forehead and reached into his pocket. Now was as good as time as any. Jake gazed at the tract and then closed it. *I'm tired of being lonely. Tired of being a lost cause.*

He opened the Gospel tract again and read it from cover to cover.

God, I've lost almost everything. I've messed up. I guess if You can change someone like Pablo, maybe there's hope for me. Forgive me. Save me. I need You. Take control of my messed up life. Show me what to do. Because I sure don't know what I'm doing. He closed his eyes, head tipped back, and drew in slow, easy breaths.

"Jake? Is that you? You all right?"

Jake opened his eyes. "Pastor Clyde?"

"I'm on my way back from the homeless shelter. Do you need a ride?"

"You could say that."

16

After a less-than-good-night's sleep, Jake crawled into his damaged car and gazed at his fingers. Still shaky. He reached for his cell phone. What exactly should he tell Detective Krouse? That he entered Randy's house and found the passport with Randy's photo, but the name Allen Jeffery Barr? That he might be connected with the APCC and working with Xavier? What crime had Randy committed exactly? And what proof did Jake have? Randy wasn't around, but other than that, what did he have to go on?

Nothing added up. Why would Randy use the name Allen Jeffery Barr? What, if anything, did that have to do with Geoffrey Walters? Were they working together?

Randy was a jokester. Could it be a prank? Entirely possible.

But why would he have all those newspaper clippings of the articles about the three missing women? Or information about the APCC. Then again, he was a journalist. Maybe he had a work-related reason.

Sure, Randy hadn't shown up for work, but was it too early to file a Missing Persons report? It seemed like the best place to start. Plus, if Randy was connected to the missing women, or had information concerning them, the police should have that information.

He dialed Detective Krouse's number and hung up. What was he waiting for? Yes, it all sounded strange. Yes, she might think he was a lunatic. He dialed again, and the call went to voicemail.

"Kelsey, it's Jake Hartman. I...uh...I need to talk to you. I think a coworker is missing, plus he's caught up in something. What I'm not sure. I'd like to talk to you rather than going directly to the station, because honestly, I don't know what's going on. You'll not believe this story. I'm having a hard time believing it myself. Please call me when you get the chance. Thanks." He released a pent-up breath. Stress could do things to people. What had he really seen?

Having lost his job and his wife, at least he didn't have to worry about his reputation being more damaged than it already was. Still, it was nice to have at least one friend who believed in him. Now, Randy was missing, and what would Krouse think of him once he talked to her? What would she say if she found out about Stu firing him and Allison's allegations against him? He was still trying to make amends for almost blowing her cover at the casino.

As a newspaper reporter, Jake lived a life based on facts, details, and stories. Too bad the facts didn't exactly paint a flattering picture of him. This story didn't seem slanted in his favor.

~*~

Carlotta sat at the kitchen table and scrolled through outfits on her laptop while she sipped her morning coffee. She'd need just the right one to wear when she and Geoffrey attended the art gala next month. Too long. Too short. Ugh. Too frilly. He could have invited any of his friends. It was kind of him to think of her.

The scent of enchiladas from the night before still permeated the room. While she may not be able to have kids, at least she could cook. A smile spread across her face.

The landline rang, and Carlotta scrambled to answer it. "Hello?"

"It's Pablo. I was released because the police dropped the charges. Anyway, I'm going to church this morning, and I wanted to know if Rosario and Antonio would come with me. You can come, too."

Released from prison. So Pablo was innocent. Maybe he really had changed. Very good news for her sister and her nephew. Carlotta lowered her voice. "She and Antonio are still sleeping, but I'll let her know you called and invited her to church. Bye."

Church. Her parents had taken her and Rosario, and maybe therein was the problem. Dad, with all his shortcomings attended, as if nothing was wrong. His infidelity drove Mom to drink. So why didn't God just smite Dad on the spot? She shivered. Despite all the bad, he was still her dad. Was that how God felt? Did He love her dad?

She and Jake had tried a local church a few times. Just for a change. Plus, it looked similar to the chapel where Jake's grandma had dragged him several Sunday mornings. If she had kids, she'd take them sometimes. All the God stuff couldn't hurt. Some of it might be useful. Things like kindness, love, serving others. A choose-your-own, cafeteria-style God and religion.

Rosario stumbled into the kitchen and scrutinized her like their parents did when she and her sister had come home past curfew. "Who was that?"

"Pablo called. He's been released. The police dropped the charges."

Rosario put her hand to her mouth.

"And he's going to church. He wants us all to go with him." Why'd she say that? She could have just left herself out. Then she could have stayed home and relaxed. Then again, if she went, maybe she could put pressure on her sister to get back together with Pablo.

"Church? Does the pastor know what Pablo's done? They're really gonna let him inside?" Rosario chuckled.

They let Dad in, and he didn't fry. "C'mon, maybe he's changed. People do." Not Dad or Jake, but maybe Pablo was an outlier.

Rosario's eyes shimmered with tears. "I have spent the past year putting up defenses against that man, and I'm not sure I'm ready to take them down. Not just yet. I can't risk getting hurt again. I have to protect myself and Antonio."

"I understand. That's why I'll go with you." Yep, she'd have to go for her sister.

She and Rosario raced around to get themselves

and Antonio ready.

An hour later, Pablo arrived.

Carlotta let him inside.

Her sister did a double take as Pablo entered the room. "This is for real. Like really real?" She studied his eyes and ran her hands up and down the sleeves of his sport coat.

Pablo arched a brow. "You like it? A friend from church gave it to me."

Rosario shook her head. "I just can't believe it. Am I dreaming?"

He grabbed Rosario's hands. "It's real, Rosie. I can't take back what happened. I can't change that. But I wanna do better for you and Antonio."

As if on cue, Antonio came into the room.

Carlotta grabbed his hand. She led him to a chair, settled into it, and set him on her lap.

Pablo handed Rosario a blue gift bag. "I brought Antonio something. But only if it's OK with you." Next, he handed her a small box.

Rosario stared at the light blue object but stopped short of opening it. "What's this?" She held it outstretched toward him.

He gently pushed the box back in her direction. "That's for you. If it's OK with you."

Rosario narrowed her gaze. "Pablo, you didn't have to…"

Pablo grinned and nodded. "Yes, I want to."

"Thank you."

"Please open it."

Her sister opened the box and held it so Carlotta

could peer inside. A gold necklace lay inside. The diamond pendant sparkled.

"Let me help you." Pablo pulled the necklace from the box and handed the empty box to Carlotta.

Rosario turned, and after gently pushing her hair aside, Pablo secured the necklace. She turned around and locked eyes with him.

Carlotta cleared her throat.

Rosario and Pablo broke their stare-down.

A few minutes later, they left for church.

Carlotta picked up the bulletin and studied it. A sermon on King David. She vaguely recalled details of his life. As a shepherd boy he fought Goliath. Later, he was crowned king.

The pastor began his sermon. During the parts when he described David's adultery with Bathsheba and later, his confrontation with the prophet Nathan, Carlotta found herself nodding. *Mmm hmm.* But wait, this man was known as a man after God's own heart. How could God forgive scum like David, Jake, and Dad? She cast a glance at Pablo. Wasn't that what she was asking her sister to do? She huffed. Different circumstances. Pablo wasn't unfaithful. He did drugs. Somewhere in her own sin hierarchy, drugs ranked lower than adultery. And yet, had she pushed him there? Things had been distant toward the end. She'd been so focused on having a child and not on her husband or their marriage.

After the service, Pablo took them back to Rosario's duplex.

Carlotta grabbed Antonio's hand. "C'mon. Let

Mommy talk for a while. You can play with Aunt Carlotta." Antonio followed her inside. She read him three stories and then stacked wooden blocks with him until Rosario joined them.

Rosario clasped a hand to her mouth.

"Are you OK?" Carlotta added another block to Antonio's tower then stood.

She nodded and lowered her voice. "Yeah, he wants to get back together. Wants to know if I'll let him move back in."

"And?"

Rosario flashed a close-lipped smile. "I told him I'd have to think about it." Rosario knelt down and began to play with Antonio.

Carlotta hummed. Soon, her sister and Pablo might be a happy family for once.

~*~

Carlotta had tried so hard not to eat regular bread in front of her sister since she'd started her new diet. Today, at the restaurant, she ate what she wanted.

Once the waitress brought her check, Carlotta paid for her brunch.

Geoffrey retrieved his credit card from his wallet and did the same. His phone rang, and he answered it. He turned to her. "I have to go to the police station. Right up the street. Would you like to go for a walk?"

"Sure." She rubbed her arms.

"Is everything OK?"

"I was thinking about those missing women. It's a

good thing I'm not walking alone."

Geoffrey held open the door.

"Thank you." Carlotta matched his pace as they walked to the police station.

"I just need to speak to someone about a client. Can you stay here a moment?" He gestured to a waiting area.

She sat in a chair.

A man in the distance scowled and spoke to a police officer. She narrowed her gaze. What was Jake doing here? Probably just reporting. Stu offered to give the crime assignments to someone else, but if she didn't know better, Jake enjoyed them. And he was good at what he did. Always found a way to write about the dead respectfully. She strained to hear.

"I was listening to the scanner. Can you tell me? Is she OK? It was her, wasn't it?" Jake asked.

Had something happened to the blonde officer?

"If she's OK, if she's here, I need to talk to her." Jake said.

About a case or something else? Had he moved on?

Geoffrey joined her. "Are you ready to go?"

"Yes." Geoffrey was just a friend. Maybe she should take Jake at his word that he wasn't dating anyone else.

Geoffrey opened the door, and Carlotta hurried outside. "I saw Jake in there. Asking about a female officer. I suppose it could be innocent. What do you think?"

"He is a reporter. I think he is concerned about

reporting the story. That is what seems to drive him."

"Yeah, he does care about families and reporting about the victims."

Geoffrey's eye twitched.

"Are you OK?"

He cleared his throat. "Yes, I think my allergies are acting up." He rubbed his eye. "Would you care to continue walking to the drugstore up the street with me?"

"No, not at all." She huffed as they continued along the sidewalk.

Two men sat on a bench across the street. They looked over at Carlotta and grinned.

She moved closer to Geoffrey's side. With women going missing, thank goodness, she had a male friend nearby.

Her mind flashed to all the true crime stories Jake had told her over the years. Those poor women. Just the thought of being held captive by some sicko… She flinched.

As they moved within several feet of the pharmacy parking lot, Geoffrey paused and smiled, his hands behind his back.

"We're almost there," Carlotta exhaled.

"Yes, I would agree." He smiled. His eye twitched again.

Thank goodness she had a friend like him. What would she do without him?

17

Light shone in through the living room window. Carlotta squinted. She'd fallen asleep on the couch reading a book and had overslept. At least she didn't have to work today.

Rosario entered the room. "I wanted to talk to you before I get ready for work and drop Antonio at Pablo's apartment."

She rubbed her eyes. "What is it?"

"Pablo thought he saw Geoffrey with that blonde from Jake's work again."

"The blonde? No, he must be mistaken." But what if it was true? That would mean Carlotta was a fool and couldn't trust herself to be a good judge of character. First Jake and now her friend Geoffrey. No, she refused to believe it.

"Just be careful. I don't want you to get hurt again."

Her mind searched for reasonable explanations. "Geoffrey's an attorney. Maybe she needed legal advice. Yes, that's right. I remember now. She accused Jake of sexual harassment."

Rosario gasped. "Jake? I mean he's outgoing and can get on my nerves, but even I wouldn't suspect that."

"Yes, Jake. Maybe it was someone who looked like her. It's not like she's the only tall, thin blonde in Cincinnati."

"You're probably right. I just wanted to let you know. I gotta get dressed and help Antonio to get ready." Rosario ambled away.

Carlotta's cell vibrated. She managed to locate it in her pocket and gazed at the number—Geoffrey's. "Hello?"

"Hello. I am home now, but I was just at the courthouse right when it opened. I got a tip. The police found evidence that links Jake to Ed's death at the animal shelter and also to the near kidnapping at Eden Park. The rumor is he sent a confession to his boss. I did not want to tell you, but I thought you should know. I would rather you hear it from me first rather than from a reporter on TV."

Carlotta clasped a hand to her mouth. "The animal shelter? I thought he was at work that evening."

Geoffrey coughed. "He interviewed the mayor that night, but he committed the crime before returning to work. A near-perfect alibi. I am sure it is hard to believe someone you once trusted, someone so close to you, could be up to something so sinister."

Carlotta shook her head. "But why?"

"From what I gather, he has some problems. But the important thing is they are his, not yours. You are not to blame. I have to go, but we can talk more later. I will see you soon. Good-bye, Carlotta."

Carlotta ended the call but tightened her grip on the phone. What caused her husband—soon-to-be-ex—

to do such a thing? If she wasn't to blame, then what or who was? Was Jake Hartman a control freak? Yes. An adulterer? Yes. But what had sent him over the edge, caused him to commit murder?

~*~

Carlotta rested in her car for another moment, studied the divorce papers in front of her, and inhaled a deep breath. She wasn't one to just up and call it quits, but he'd committed adultery. And apparently murder. Kidnapping, too? And who knew what other crimes. No chance for reconciliation at this point. It was over. She grabbed a pen from her middle console and signed the papers, careful not to leave anything blank. Reaching over to the passenger seat, she retrieved a manila envelope, placed the divorce papers inside, and returned the pen to the console. At least she could put things away. Something that Jake failed to learn.

Enough about Jake. Carlotta grabbed the envelope and her purse, approached the door to Geoffrey's home, and knocked. No answer, but a slight gust of wind blew the door slightly ajar. She opened it with care.

The police would arrest Jake, but he could have an accomplice. What if there was another psychopath on the loose? How long would Jake be in prison? What if he got out and wanted to come after her? Everything was confusing.

What if the accomplice had gotten to Geoffrey?

Jake was jealous enough to send those creepy notes and flowers. He'd killed Ed and almost kidnapped a jogger. He was mad about a photo of Geoffrey and her. He could have hired someone to go after her or Geoffrey.

Carlotta stepped inside the old home. She set down her purse and the manila envelope on a small table in the foyer. Then she held her keys between the fingers of one hand, ready to be used as a weapon. Breathe. She backed up against the wall and inched along the hallway leading to the bathroom and bedrooms. The light was off in the bathroom. She flipped the switch. Her heart raced. No one in sight. Stepping closer to the shower, she inhaled and then peeled back the curtain. No one. She began to exhale but shuddered as she stared in the mirror. Like a scene in a horror flick, she expected a face to appear behind her image.

She left the bathroom and continued toward the master bedroom. With a lunge toward the bedroom door, she flicked on the light and then jumped back. The room was empty. "Geoffrey? I signed the papers and brought them over for you. Geoffrey?"

She opened the closet. Just clothes.

What about the bed? She knelt down, flipped up the comforter, and peered underneath. Nothing. Carlotta was about to stand, but something blue caught her eye. Plastic bed sheets. What had Jake said about psychopaths and bedwetting?

"Looking for something?"

Carlotta jumped. "You're OK. Thank goodness.

The door was open. I was afraid... that something happened to you." Carlotta slid her cell phone in her back pocket, stood, and faced Geoffrey.

As Geoffrey stood and stepped closer, Carlotta's heart skipped a beat, and not in a good way. "The door was open. I thought someone had broken into your house."

"Sorry, I had stepped outside to water the plants in the backyard. The wind must have blown the door open. I need to have a carpenter look at that doorjamb."

Carlotta stole a quick glance at the bed sheets. Merely coincidence. Had to be. Or maybe they weren't plastic. *I've been under a lot of stress lately. Better not jump to conclusions.* "I signed the papers. They're on the table. Geoffrey..." She started to cry.

"What is it?"

"My mind keeps racing. What if Jake gets out? What if he hurts you or me or..."

"Shhh...It will be OK."

Her mind flashed back to when she was younger and her Mom had been drunk. Nope, don't go there. Safe—that's what she was now.

18

Jake relaxed his shoulders, sighed, and propped his bare feet on the coffee table. He drew his lips upward into a smile. If Carlotta had been there, she'd have chided him. He huffed. Too bad she wasn't. And yet, right now, a little scolding from her might be nice. His phone vibrated, and he swung his feet onto the floor. He dug his toes into the carpet for a minute and then retrieved his cell phone from his pants pocket.

A new text message from Allison.

I hope you're happy. I'm pregnant.

His jaw dropped. She got him fired and then wanted to let him know she was having a baby. What was this about? Money? For the baby or for an abortion?

Jake winced. Allison a mother, but not Carlotta. *Why, God?*

His phone chimed. Another message from Allison.

Meet me at my place. We need to discuss this like two adults.

The first sane idea she'd had since he didn't know when. Maybe motherhood would force her to do some growing up. If that were possible.

Jake's fingers fumbled as he texted.

Be there in a few minutes.

Allison wouldn't attempt to throw herself at him again, would she? He stared at his phone for a minute. Maybe he should meet her somewhere public or take someone else along with him.

R U Coming, or R U abandoning me? I have an appt. with OBGYN. Want you to meet me here so we can go together.

If she really was pregnant, he'd need to step up and support her—do the right thing. He'd need to be a father to this baby and also find another job to support the child. His child.

But what if she didn't want it? He didn't like the idea of abortion, couldn't wrap his head around it. And while he was learning more and more about God—really getting to know Him—He didn't figure it'd be something God would want either. Legally, Allison could do what she wanted without his consent, but he wouldn't coerce her to terminate the pregnancy. He wasn't married to her, but he'd still help out however he could in raising the child...as much as she would allow him to be involved.

She'd mentioned an OBGYN, so maybe that was a good sign she'd want to keep the child. He rubbed his chin. The baby...what would Carlotta do when she found out? This might send her into more of a downward spiral. All of this...it was never his intention. One night of dinner and drinks. And then this. He'd only gone to talk with her. Just to talk, nothing more.

He texted his response.

Be there in 5.

Jake hopped in his car. The drive seemed shorter than he'd remembered. He knocked with caution on the door to Allison's condo.

She opened it. A dazed look spread across her face. "You came! Come in."

Jake stepped inside the doorway, and Allison motioned to the living room. Two glasses of water sat atop the coffee table. She handed him one. "Here."

Allison grabbed one of her own then sat. "I've heard they do urine testing at each appointment, so I've decided to be prepared." She took a gulp from her glass and continued to chug the water.

He sat and forced a smile and then drank some of the liquid. "Should we be going?"

Allison's eyes widened. "No, we have plenty of time."

Jake glanced at the clock on the wall. "Oh, but I thought we were in a hurry."

"I...I just wanted to make sure you weren't late, and that you'd show up."

"Oh." He drank more of the water while she excused herself momentarily. Tasted a little different, but he'd seen her drink flavored water before. Probably one of those. Still, he was parched, so he wouldn't complain. He set down the glass and glanced at his watch. "Allison?"

"I'll be out in a few minutes."

Minutes passed. He forced his eyelids to stay open. His head spun, and his muscles went limp. He reclined on the couch.

Things were kind of...like that night he'd spent

with her. When apparently, they'd had too many drinks. But this...how was? He shook his head. No, this was much worse.

Allison re-entered the room. Laughter flowed from her lips. She looked distorted, like a strange nightmare. One from which he quickly needed to escape, but how?

Two men entered Allison's apartment. She pointed at Jake and then looked back at the taller of the two. "Put him in the car. Drive to her sister's apartment and leave him outside. Then call 9-1-1."

The man nodded.

"One more thing. I only roofied him. But make sure they find this on him. Let them think he's a druggie." She handed the shorter man a bottle of pills. He put them in his pocket.

The taller rubbed his chin. "I thought you wanted to kill him."

She shook her head. "Not yet. I want him to suffer some more first. Get revenge."

The shorter man grabbed his shoulders while the taller man grabbed Jake's legs and flashed him a wicked grin. He winked at Allison. "Anything for you, sweetheart."

Where were they taking him? What had Allison done to him? Revenge for what? Hadn't he suffered enough? *Lord, please help me. Protect me.*

~*~

Jake opened his eyes. He wasn't dead, just in a hospital. His gaze landed on the nurse by the side of his bed.

"Hello, Mr. Hartman." She glanced at her watch and avoided eye contact.

What had happened? Allison must have slipped something in his drink. Whew, at least the police were here. Something finally good out of all this mess.

Detective Hadley entered the room and stepped toward the nurse. "How much longer does he need to stay?"

"Based on the pills you found, we suspected an overdose, but no traces of drugs were found in his system. He can leave." She handed him several papers. "Here's the discharge paperwork."

She'd probably roofied him. Both now and before. That explained why he couldn't remember the night in question. Should he speak up? No, he'd better keep his mouth shut for now. Might be better to have a lawyer present.

Hadley approached Jake's bed. "Sorry, but we're just doing our job. Jake Hartman. You are under arrest…"

Jake's chin trembled. "For what?"

Hadley helped him up. "We have your signed confession and evidence that ties you to a crime scene."

His pulse raced. He met Detective Krouse's gaze for a second, and then his look shifted to his hospital gown.

"Get dressed," Hadley said.

Krouse turned around.

Once Jake put on his clothes, Hadley cuffed him from behind.

Time slowed. Things went silent.

"This way." Hadley led him down the hospital corridor and outside to the police vehicle.

Krouse followed behind. What must she think of him?

Jake blinked rapidly. Hadley helped him inside the vehicle.

Krouse sat in the passenger seat, cast a quick glance at him, and then turned away.

Jake sighed. Carlotta would become even closer to the creep in his absence. Jake couldn't protect her from jail. Who would believe him now? Not when he'd be labeled a criminal. He clenched his fists against the cold metal of the handcuffs. Maybe it would have been better if Allison had done him in. He choked back a sob. Nope, God was with him. He couldn't think like that. If only he could explain things to the police. Let's face it. If he were them, he'd think he was guilty, too.

Krouse cleared her throat.

What would Krouse do? Probably pray.

God, I've lost my job, my wife, and probably my freedom, too. All I have is You. Please help me.

~*~

The doorbell rang. Geoffrey stared at her and sighed. "Be right back. Let me see who it is."

Carlotta ambled in the opposite direction. "Take your time. I need to use the bathroom." She entered the hallway bathroom and gazed at the toilet paper holder. Empty. She looked under the sink. No spare rolls? She peeked outside the bathroom and cast a glance down the hallway.

Geoffrey was still outside talking to someone. No reason to bother him. Carlotta scampered to his bedroom and inside his bathroom. She searched for toilet paper under the cabinet. Voila. Carlotta grabbed a roll. Beep. She located the source of the noise. Geoffrey must have left his phone next to the sink when he came home. After putting it in her pocket, she hurried back out to the hallway.

Geoffrey was still busy.

Nature called. No time to set down the phone. She ran to the hall bathroom with the phone in her pocket and the toilet paper. After she washed and dried her hands, a beep sounded. And another. She removed the phone from her pocket. A text message popped up. From Allison? So he knew her? There had to be a reason. A good one.

I finished drugging him and put him in front of her sister's house. He's probably in police custody by now. Are you sure you don't want to just get rid of her now?

Her legs grew weak, and her pulse raced.

"Carlotta?"

He'd find her. Then what? She retrieved her cell from her pocket and sent a message to Rosario.

Geoffrey is a murderer. He's trying to hurt Jake, and he's going to hurt me. I'm at his house. Please call the police."

Her fingers trembled as she placed the phone back in her pocket. "Almost finished." Maybe she should just stay in the bathroom until the police arrived. Yeah, but he would get suspicious and probably just break down the door. No, she could play it cool until he arrived. She stuffed Geoffrey's phone in her other pocket. Carlotta inhaled a deep breath then opened the bathroom door.

Geoffrey's gaze met hers. "Is everything OK?"

She shifted her gaze to the floor. "Yes, um...who were you talking to?"

Geoffrey shrugged. "Just a solicitor. I need to put up one of those no soliciting signs. Sheesh, some people will try to sell you anything."

A beep sounded. His gaze landed on her pocket.

"Oh, I was looking for toilet paper and found your phone by the sink. Here." She handed it to him.

He stuffed the phone in his pocket. "Are you sure you are OK?"

Carlotta rubbed her neck with one hand. "I just need some fresh air. Can we go outside?"

"Sure." Geoffrey opened the sliding glass door. He sat down at the patio table, and she paced around the yard. How much longer until the police arrived? She ambled across his lawn, putting distance between the two of them.

"I'm thirsty. Would you like me to get you some water, too?" he asked.

"No, thank you."

Geoffrey went back inside.

She swallowed hard. This might be her only chance. She scurried to the corner gate. A padlock adorned the gate lock. Wait, there was another gate. Over by the garage. She jogged over to examine the second gate. It was older and overgrown by ivy. Carlotta pushed some of the ivy out of the way. No lock. This was her chance. Her shoulders relaxed and then tensed as a hand clasped her mouth.

"Shhhh. I see I have a text message that was read before I opened it."

"What did you do to Jake?" She clawed at his hand, but he held onto her tighter.

"Tsk. Tsk. You should have minded your business. And Jake, he'll get what he deserves...my revenge."

Sirens sounded in the distance.

He grabbed her wrist and spun her around to face him. "What have you done?" Geoffrey strengthened his grip, opened the gate, and marched her out back to his car.

Carlotta gasped. Revenge for what? She'd been mad at Jake for committing adultery. How mad must Geoffrey be to be willing to commit murder? What had Jake done, or what did Geoffrey think he did? Jake reported the news. Maybe a story Geoffrey really didn't like.

Geoffrey removed a pistol from his pocket, pushed the barrel against the small of Carlotta's back, and forced her in the vehicle. Once inside, he zip-tied her wrists.

Her heart raced. "You're hurting me."

"Yes, but also Jake." Geoffrey took off down the alley. His eyes exuded a coldness she'd never experienced before.

Carlotta eyed the door lock. Her heartbeat thrashed in her ears. Could she reach for the door lock with her hands tied? And then what? Try to jump out while the car moved? What if he shot her? Then again, he planned on killing her, anyway.

19

A call came over the police radio. Jake was familiar with a few law enforcement codes but wasn't sure what was taking place. Something lively from the looks on Detective Hadley's face.

The detective called into the station and then turned to Detective Krouse. "Carlotta Hartman."

Jake clenched his jaw. What had happened to his wife?

Hadley clucked his tongue, turned the car around, and headed in the opposite direction.

Dare he ask them what was happening? His mind flashed to the butchered dogs at the animal shelter. Had Geoffrey hurt Carlotta? *Please, God, no.* He made a mental inventory of landmarks along the way. As best as he could tell, they approached the Hyde Park neighborhood. *C'mon. Why can't he drive any faster?* Jake took a deep breath. The police were doing their best. Yelling at them wouldn't help. Detective Krouse was a fair person. She and Hadley had only arrested him based on planted evidence. Now, they would try to help his wife. Time to relax and work with the police, not against them.

Hadley pulled up to a Victorian house, complete with gingerbread woodwork and parked on the street.

Several officers walked around the property.

Both officers emerged from the car and headed toward the house, leaving Jake cuffed and locked inside. He peered out the window. Carlotta's car sat in the driveway. Maybe she was inside talking with police. Jake released a pent-up breath.

Was this where Geoffrey lived? Manicured topiaries lined the front. Jake snickered. Such a beautiful house and property for such an evil man. What was that he'd heard his granny say once? That Satan masqueraded as an angel of light?

He leaned back against the seat. Stuck in a car. Wanted for crimes he didn't commit. Meanwhile, a madman had befriended his wife. *Be strong and of good courage. God is with you wherever you go.*

Jake slumped his shoulders. For much of his life, he'd tried to do things on his own. For once, Jake had no other choice but to trust God. His problems were beyond his control. He huffed. And who better to handle his concerns? The Creator of the universe. Why was it he thought he could do better than God in the first place? He shook his head. Pride.

If he and Carlotta ever moved past this, he'd live more humbly. What if Jake did have to go to prison? Well, that sure would bring some humility. Regardless, God was in control. He had a plan, a purpose for Jake's life.

~*~

Detective Krouse jogged inside the house with the

other detective close to her heels. If this man, this monster, had kidnapped Jake's wife, it stood to reason he'd be the same kind to set up her friend. And she was fixin' to exonerate him.

Krouse stood defensively and followed Hadley. He advanced toward a bedroom and motioned for her to check out a second room.

She tiptoed inside. No signs of Geoffrey or Carlotta. Crouching, she checked under the bed. Only one more spot, the closet. Krouse used one hand to hold her pistol and the other to slide open the closet door. Boxes stared back at her. No sign of Carlotta or Geoffrey.

Taking another glance around the closet, she spied notes and photos tacked to a bulletin board. Perhaps a clue as to Carlotta's whereabouts. Creeping closer, she studied them.

Photos of a dead man at the animal shelter. Presumably taken by the killer himself. Photos of a younger man who had been gagged and had his hands bound. Krouse inspected it again. Didn't he work with Jake? She nodded. Yep, he'd been missing. Add kidnapping to murder. Hopefully, the victim was still alive. Receipts for a florist? Photos of the jogger in the park. Photos of Carlotta Hartman, too. Wait, some of Carlotta and Jake, probably before they separated. She glanced at the desk to the side of the bulletin board. Baggies with a hairbrush and toothbrush inside labeled Jake Hartman. Notes on planting DNA.

Detective Hadley put a hand on her shoulder. "What is all this?"

"Looks like Geoffrey Walters fabricated and planted the evidence on Jake. If that's true, we have nothing to hold him on. We'll need to talk to a judge."

Hadley clucked his tongue and nodded. "I'll write out an affidavit for a search warrant."

She shivered. A suspect so daring and proud he displayed the evidence like a trophy.

A cold, strange feeling overcame her. She'd sensed it once before at another crime scene, a particularly horrific one. If she had to put a name to it, it'd be *evil*. Krouse didn't believe in ghosts, but she believed in God, and in right and wrong. Right now, she couldn't help but feel she stood in the presence of something sinister. *Protect me, Father, and Hadley. And Jake. Let the truth come out. Protect Jake's wife. Help us catch this monster.* Detective Krouse headed toward the front door of the house.

"I'll contact the judge." Krouse trekked toward the car. A wave of relief swept over her. She hadn't misjudged Jake. Maybe she wasn't such a bad judge of character after all.

~*~

Good thing Jake had made friends with Judge Raines over the years, and even better the judge made time that afternoon to sign the search warrant, review the evidence, and to release him. Detective Krouse referred to it as a 'God thing.' Otherwise, Jake might have remained in police custody longer. He gritted his teeth. Still, he'd wasted several hours. What had happened to Carlotta during that time? He blew out a breath. *Please watch over her.*

Krouse escorted Jake out of the courtroom. "You were set up."

He nodded. "Drugged, too, by Allison Console. She's working with him. I don't know the connection."

"Hmmm."

"Geoffrey is friends with Carlotta, but for all I know, he could be dating Allison. She once mentioned revenge as a motive. But for what, I don't know. Maybe I investigated something or reported on something they didn't like." Jake retrieved his phone from his pocket and sent a text. "There, I texted you her phone number and address. So where's Carlotta?"

Detective Hadley avoided eye contact. "You are free to go, Mr. Hartman. I'm sorry, but we haven't found your wife yet. But we won't stop looking. I'll let you know if we find anything. Take care."

"Thank you." Jake trudged down the sidewalk until he came to a bench and sat down. He called for a cab and then received a text.

Ghostly twin tunnels lie under the Rhine, and also a centaur hidden in time. Come alone to Hopple Street. Or an untimely death your wife will soon meet.

He held his breath. How did Geoffrey know the police had released him, unless... Was there at least one dirty cop on the inside, someone helping Geoffrey? Or perhaps, as an attorney, he'd used his law enforcement connections to pry information?

His phone dinged again. Another text from Geoffrey.

Leave your phone at home.

The creep had taken her, but where?

Come alone. Leave your phone at home.

Without knowing Geoffrey's connection, and the tools of surveillance he might have at his disposal, Jake couldn't involve the police. And he'd leave his phone at home. If they knew he had it, Carlotta's life wouldn't be worth anything. He shook his head as he reread the text. A riddle. Folklore. Randy would have been good at solving this. Had Geoffrey and Allison killed him, too? Or was he involved?

Twin tunnels? The Rhine...that was a river. Over the Rhine was a neighborhood in Cincinnati. But this was "under the Rhine." Under? Like a cemetery? A hidden centaur? Hopple Street. Hmm...where was that?

Jake opened a browser on his phone and typed "twin tunnels under the Rhine centaur Hopple Street. He scanned the results. Hopple Street Tunnel? An abandoned part of the Cincinnati Subway? The tunnels. He'd forgotten about them. Mostly because the subway never went through. Guess he should have gone on that tour with Randy back when he'd offered.

He bit his lip. Should he text Krouse and Hadley and let them know what was up?

The taxi cab's wheels screeched as the driver braked.

Jake climbed inside. After giving the cabbie directions to his house, he continued to read the search results. Caverns that stretched over two miles under Central Parkway. More tunnels under Hopple Street.

Twenty-five thousand square feet of black nothingness. A dark, secluded underground location. Alone. He squirmed. Then his gaze shifted outside the window to a large church with stained glass windows. Nope, never alone. God was with Him.

Jake stepped out of the taxi and paid the cabbie his fare. He stood and stared at his house for a moment. It was a wonder Geoffrey and Allison hadn't tried to burn it down yet. What would he need to wage battle in the dark? Light. Lots of it. He needed to make sure he had that, but first, he needed to print out Geoffrey's clue.

After driving into town to an army surplus store, Jake bought night vision goggles and then hurried back home. Jake studied the goggles. *I'm just a journalist, not a Navy Seal. What am I doing?*

He'd been home for about five minutes when the doorbell rang. He stashed the night goggles in a kitchen drawer and answered the front door. "Hello."

Detectives Krouse and Hadley stood outside. Had they found Carlotta already? Why didn't they just call? They were there in person. Did that mean something bad had happened, and they'd come to break the news to him?

Jake opened the door and gestured. "Come on in."

Both detectives stepped inside. "We're still looking for your wife," Hadley said. "We believe Geoffrey Walters kidnapped her. With her car outside, and her not at his house, and his vehicle missing, we believe he's taken her somewhere."

"Do you have any recent photos of your wife we

may use? Also, any items of clothing we can give to a bloodhound?" Krouse asked.

To find her alive or to identify a body? *Please let her be alive, God.*

"She hasn't stayed here recently, but she left behind some coats. Follow me."

Krouse followed Jake into his bedroom.

Detective Hadley stayed behind on the couch.

Jake gave Krouse some photos and two jackets that belonged to Carlotta.

"They're all here except one. She must have taken one with her. It's dark green. The hood has fur on it."

Krouse gave an understanding nod. "We'll do our best to find her, Jake."

"I know."

Both detectives went outside.

Jake waited until they pulled out of the driveway before grabbing his night vision goggles and shrugging on a fishing vest with large pockets. Should he have told them about the text? No, Geoffrey had warned him. *Come alone.*

~*~

Krouse got into the car.

Hadley started the vehicle and drove away from Jake Hartman's house. He turned toward her. "I hate to tell you, but Jake isn't being completely forthcoming."

She tilted her head to one side and pursed her lips. "What do you mean?"

"I found this on his counter." He kept one hand on

the wheel, and when he stopped at the nearest stop sign, he handed her his cell phone.

Krouse looked at the photo. "A poem?"

Hadley shrugged. "He had a printout of a text message. I took a photo. Maybe the message is from Walters. Can't blame him for not saying anything though. It's his wife, and Walters instructed him to come alone and threatened him if he didn't. Fear can cause people to make poor decisions."

She read the poem. "Ghostly twin tunnels lie under the Rhine, and also a centaur hidden in time. Come alone to Hopple Street. Or an untimely death your wife will soon meet." *Please, God, help us find this woman.*

Hadley knitted his brows. "Under the Rhine? Twin tunnels?"

"Maybe underpasses?"

"Perhaps. Are there any near the Over the Rhine neighborhood?"

Krouse looked out the window and stared at nothing in particular. "Oh, I'm sure there are probably a few. Guess we'll have to drive around and check each one."

"There's that underground nightclub."

"Would he take her to a public place? Wait, didn't it mention a centaur? Maybe that's a clue, too." Krouse reread the poem. "It also mentions Hopple Street. Wait…." Detective Krouse's jaw dropped. "The old subway."

Hadley's eyes widened. "Hopple Street Tunnel. Over by Central Parkway. Let's go."

Hadley looked as though he'd seen a ghost.

"You OK?" she asked.

"Just the thought of that place gives me the heebie jeebies. It takes a lot to do that. Which is saying something. Let's head over there but definitely call for back up." He opened his mouth and then closed it. "Look, I know you believe in God. Maybe now's the time to pray or something."

"Oh, I've been praying. Believe me."

20

Geoffrey drove Carlotta to a secluded location. He led her out of the car. She glanced at the wooded terrain surrounding her. The forest foliage was a welcome contrast to the interior of the madman's vehicle. Carlotta studied the landscape. No hikers in sight.

She inhaled fresh air and then swallowed hard. The blonde from Jake's workplace—Allison—stepped out of the car and flashed a devilish grin. *What did Jake ever see in that woman?*

"Can't have you signaling to other people." Geoffrey gripped Carlotta's arm, and he and Allison began to stuff her in the trunk of his car. *Oh, no, you don't.* Carlotta kicked.

Allison's hand connected with her face. Shocked, and with a stinging cheek, she fell back into the trunk. Geoffrey appeared to yell at Allison as she slammed the trunk shut.

Carlotta tried to kick out a brake light, but it was no use. For now, she'd conserve her strength. They drove around for what felt like hours.

Now what? The car had stopped. Geoffrey helped her out. Where were they? Some buildings set in the distance. Had they returned to the city?

Geoffrey slid wraparound sunglasses on her face. But not regular ones. These let no light inside. Before a scream could escape Carlotta's lips, a weapon pushed against her back.

"Quick, before someone sees us," Allison said. "I don't think it was a good idea to do this during the daytime."

Vehicle noises. Hmm... Carlotta could run. Geoffrey might shoot her, or a car might hit her, but better than whatever Geoffrey had in mind.

Carlotta bolted, and someone tugged her backward. Another body pushed against her other side. "Nice try," Allison whispered.

Geoffrey said. "Step up."

Sucking in a breath, Carlotta's foot moved up onto presumably the curb. Had they crossed the street? Now where were they going?

As the two of them shoved her along, Carlotta flinched. Pablo said he'd seen Geoffrey and Allison together. So was this really some plan to get back at Jake for publishing a story? There'd been some pipe bombs at the newspaper office. Maybe they were mad at the paper. But why take it out on Jake specifically? Why not Stu, his boss, or the owner of the newspaper?

"Watch your step." Geoffrey said. Traffic noise still sounded, but not as loud as before. They were moving away from the street. Away from people and civilization.

Something crunched under Carlotta's shoes. Glass, maybe? Something brushed against her. Were they in a wooded area?

"Through here." Geoffrey pushed Carlotta downward and though something. Metal scraped against her skin. Where were they?

They'd stopped. Now what?

"We're here," Geoffrey said.

They were inside somewhere. The ground underneath her shoes had been replaced with concrete. It was cold. Even with the dark sunglasses on, it was darker than before. Dark and cold. Where were they? A cave? No, there were no caves in the middle of the city. They stumbled along for quite a while before Geoffrey removed her sunglasses.

Darkness surrounded them. Were they in a basement? The scent of urine, along with a general moldy, damp scent assaulted her nose. Suspicious noises—squeaking and scurrying—sounded in the background. Rats, snakes, spiders, anything could be here.

If Geoffrey hadn't bound her hands, she'd wrap them around herself for warmth. He pushed her into a chair then bound her ankles. Carlotta closed her eyes. She should have tried to escape while she was in the car. How would she get out of here now?

He held a small floodlight. "Tsk, tsk, Carlotta. You were so upset that you killed yourself, just slit your wrists over Jake." Geoffrey shook his head. "So rash."

Carlotta shivered. What was he talking about? What if she died down here, and the rats feasted on her body? Would anyone find her or know what happened to her?

Allison came into view. "Is this where you want

them to find the body?"

Geoffrey nodded at Allison.

Bile rose in Carlotta's throat. Jake had warned her, said he hadn't sent the threatening notes. But the florist said otherwise. Would Geoffrey have paid the florist to lie? She wouldn't put anything past him now. How had she allowed herself to be fooled by such a person?

Allison stepped closer to Carlotta. Light glinted off a razor in her hand.

Carlotta avoided flinching, gulped down a breath.

Geoffrey grabbed Allison's arm. "Journalists like Jake have material that isn't ready to be made public yet. They call it hold for release. Carlotta is like that. I am not ready for her to die yet. This is why I call the shots, remember? One of us had to be the brains of the operation."

"And thank you for always reminding me." Allison scurried away with the floodlight and disappeared into the darkness.

Carlotta scanned her surroundings. Cold and dark. The blackness stretched for miles. Basically, a cave in the middle of Cincinnati. With a killer and his accomplice. She felt the rise of dread and hyperventilated for a few seconds. No one would save her. She had to keep her wits and her panic down on her own. It took all the willpower she had to alter her breathing to compensate.

Geoffrey said he would wait to kill her, that he wanted Jake to suffer. That meant there was still time to escape.

~*~

Jake parked near Hopple Street. He bolted out of his car and removed a large metal flashlight from the trunk, stuffing it in one of the fishing vest pockets. In another pocket, he stashed the night vision goggles. He looked both ways.

A hand tugged his arm. He looked over at a young man holding a clipboard. "Can you sign this petition, please? We're trying to—."

"I'm sorry, I don't have time." Jake stepped forward.

The man moved along his side. "I promise I'll only take a minute of your time."

"Sorry, I can't."

The guy grabbed Jake's arm. "C'mon, man. I just need a few more signatures."

Jake turned around and took on a forceful tone. "I said no."

As he marched ahead, the man huffed. "Whatever. I'll find someone else."

After Jake jetted across Central Parkway, he approached a chain link fence. Now what? He hadn't brought cutters. He studied the fence. Someone else had made a hole. With his left hand, he tugged on the metal to allow enough room for him to pass through.

Traffic noise roared in the distance as Jake trudged through stands of weeds. He tripped on a broken bottle, fell toward a pile of trash, but righted himself. Yikes. Where was the entrance? Was this even the right place?

Geoffrey had said he'd kill Carlotta. Jake's chest tingled.

As he fought through foliage toward the tunnel, a bucket came into view. Some sort of writing on the side. And an old book lay on top. Glass crunched beneath his shoes. Good thing he'd worn some today. He picked up the book. A Bible? How long had that been there? If he hadn't been pressed for time, he might have stopped to read for encouragement.

Jake removed the night vision goggles from one pocket and put them on. From his other pocket, he removed his flashlight. He scrambled inside the tunnel. Flipping on the night vision, he shuddered. Slight movements skittered near the ground. Probably rodents of some sort. A few hypodermic needles littered the floor.

Something rubbed against his head. He touched his temple. Maybe spider webs. Jake wiped it against his clothes and continued deeper into the dark tunnel.

He steadied his breath. Who knew what he might find down here? Homeless people? Gangs? Not to mention the psycho who had abducted his wife.

Yep, she was still his. And he aimed to keep it that way. He crept farther inside the building. What little daylight entered the area illuminated the graffiti that littered the walls. Fancy lettering in red and black wrapped around the cement columns of this dank dungeon. This place had been abandoned and off limits for a reason.

~*~

Carlotta's bones ached as she struggled against the plastic zip ties. *Careful. Don't let him see. What was that novel where the heroine escaped from ties by maneuvering her wrists just so?* If only she could remember... Or someone showed up to help.

With Jake in custody, how could he find her? After Rosario's call to the police, hopefully, they'd release him. But Geoffrey mentioned Jake dying. She wouldn't put it past Geoffrey to stage a death, even in prison. Jake had warned her about Geoffrey having a network of helpers. If only she'd listened to him. *Why did I doubt him?*

Geoffrey moved closer to her, appeared to stare at nothing in particular. "I was there."

"Where?"

He jerked his head closer to her, made a fake gun gesture using his thumb and index finger, pressed the weapon against his head, and fired. "I was there at the house when he shot himself."

What was he talking about? None of this made sense. Surely, he didn't mean Jake, right? She turned her head away from him. "Who?"

He moved closer and stared at her. A twisted grin spread across his face. "Dad."

Yikes. No wonder this man had problems. Yet he was good at hiding them for so long. "I'm sorry..."

Geoffrey put a finger to her lips, and Carlotta recoiled. Her skin tightened as a creepy crawly sensation spread throughout her body.

"Not all of it is bad. Jake helped make me who I am today. The hate...it fueled me. The rage...I just wanted to see what it was like to hurt others. It was a rush. The darkness consumed me and controlled me. It pulled me in, deeper and deeper. Crushing an animal here or there. Moving up the food chain, until I dared to satisfy my curiosity to snuff out a human. Then Ed had to ruin things by having a heart attack before I could even continue my plan." Geoffrey punched the wall. A curse flew from his lips. "Completely ruined everything. I had everything planned, everything timed. The way I wanted it. It was supposed to be special." Geoffrey caressed her cheek. She tried to move away. "Like this. This time, I will get things right. I will make Jake suffer for what he's done. I'll get revenge."

His phone rang, the chime echoing in the darkness past the floodlight.

Geoffrey sauntered a few feet away.

Carlotta strained to hear his end of the conversation. Was he about to kill her now? How much longer would Geoffrey and Allison allow her to live? Death, OK, everyone died. But she didn't want to suffer.

"What do you mean you think there might be some police? Is there a police car or not?" He growled. "You are completely incompetent. Wait for me. I will be there in a few minutes." Geoffrey sighed and cast a glance at Carlotta. "And this is why you cannot count on others to do things for you. Right, Carlotta? Well, no need to worry. I will not leave you alone." He walked away in the darkness and returned with a clear container. He removed two tarantulas from a container and placed them on Carlotta's lap.

Trying to tap into her fear of bugs, eh? Carlotta squirmed as the furry arachnids crawled over her body. Her hands trembled, and she averted her gaze from the spiders, her fear barely under control. She had to stay strong, work on her escape.

Jake was right about her need for control. She hadn't counted on others. Only herself. And look where she'd ended up. So much for the appearance of control. A cold shiver swept over her. Control—only one person who had that now, and it wasn't her. The tarantulas continued to crawl about, one brushed across her arm. She bit her tongue to keep from screaming.

Geoffrey hurried away, taking the flashlight with him.

The last bit of light faded. Total darkness. Terror swamped Carlotta's soul. *Oh, Jesus, please help me…*

Dear God, help me. If they will kill me, let it be quick. Had it been quick for Jake? *Lord, I'm so sorry.*

Yes, God had given them divorce because the hearts of humans were so hard, but He still hated it. It wasn't His plan. She'd signed the divorce papers, but she didn't have to, especially when Jake wanted to make things right. It didn't mean she had the right to get revenge on him, to hurt him, to push away God.

Through the battle with infertility, on long gloomy nights, she'd questioned God's existence. If she made it through this alive, she vowed to get to know Him and not just the parts about Him and His Word with which she was comfortable. Really know Him as more than just fire insurance for the afterlife.

~*~

Jake hid behind a pillar in the darkness as two humans showed up on his night vision goggles followed by smaller lights. Maybe flashlights? They jogged closer to the entrance. Probably Geoffrey and Allison. But where was Carlotta? *Help me, God. Please give me another chance to make things right with my wife. Keep her safe. I don't care what happens to me, but let her live. Let her know You love her because I haven't done the best job of demonstrating that to her.*

Crime scenes. Gruesome accidents. Jake had witnessed his share of horrible things while reporting for the paper, but he braced himself for what he might find. He paused until he'd put some distance between himself and the other figures in the darkness. Besides, he was venturing in the opposite direction. Hopefully, they wouldn't notice.

The darkness went on for what seemed forever. *C'mon, God. I can't do this on my own. Help me out.*

An image came into view. A mattress probably used by vagrants. "Ohhh." Yikes. Apparently still used by someone who rolled over and moaned again.

He kept going. How long had he been walking? He blinked rapidly, looking all around him.

Maybe she wasn't even in here. Perhaps he should turn around. Wait, what was that?

He spied a person in the distance. Was that his wife? Was she alive? He lowered his voice. "Carly?"

No answer. "Carly!"

"Jake?" A whisper emanated. "I'm over here. They're gone. They've been gone for a little while. Allison called Geoffrey. They think they saw some police outside. Are you OK?"

His heart pounded. She was alive. *Thank You, God.* More importantly, the creep was not there.

He came closer and flicked on his flashlight. His breath burst in and out.

Carlotta sat with her hands and ankles bound. Her eyes held terror, but her jaw was clenched tight. His wife, the love of his life, was hanging on through fear by sheer, iron willpower. His heart nearly exploded with pride in her.

A movement near her neck nearly made him scream like a girl. Jake thwacked the tarantula off Carlotta's shoulder. He brushed another arachnid from her lap. "How many...?" He asked in a horrified tone.

"Only two." Her voice was thready.

Jake took a moment to put his hands on her shoulders, grip firm. "I'm here." He took a moment to examine her for injuries. "I'm here to rescue you, baby." He fought the urge to kiss her. Would she welcome one at this point? He'd better wait. "I hope the police are here. We need to put Geoffrey and Allison behind bars."

"He wants to kill me, Jake. Kill you, too. He said...you were going to die. They talked about where they would leave...my body." Carlotta's voice broke, her shoulders drooped, and she sobbed.

Jake raked his fingers through Carlotta's hair.

"Shh, baby. It'll be OK. I asked God to watch over us."

"I prayed, and He brought you here to rescue me. Jake, I don't want to get a divorce…"

He pressed his lips against hers and kissed his wife with intensity.

Footsteps sounded. A small flood light switched on, and Geoffrey came into view, pointing a pistol at them. "How touching. Think of it this way. You will die as husband and wife."

Pain spreading through his chest, Jake positioned himself in front of Carlotta and shielded her. "You want me, right?" This might be his last chance to show Carlotta how much he loved her. He was right with God. If he died, he knew where he was headed. The verse from Joshua flooded his mind. *Be of good courage. Strengthen me, God.*

This was it. What if it went off? What if it hit Carlotta? His heartbeat thrashed in his ears.

With a sudden burst of stamina, Jake reached for Geoffrey's pistol and shoved the barrel away from him and Carlotta. Using his left hand, he hit Geoffrey in the head with his flashlight.

Geoffrey winced and stretched his hand toward the sore spot.

Now or never, Jake reached for the gun again. He wrapped his hands around it.

"Jake," Carlotta screamed. "Watch out!"

Someone pressed an object against the back of Jake's head. As his brain registered what happened, Geoffrey snatched the pistol away from Jake.

"So pathetic." Allison's voice came from behind

him.

Geoffrey grunted and again pointed his gun at Jake.

Jake stepped back. Gruesome crime scene memories from his years of reporting flooded his mind. Only now, he and Carlotta would be the victims.

"How pitiful," Geoffrey sneered. "So much for your heroics."

Please, God. We need a miracle.

Geoffrey turned to Allison. "Tons of homeless people down here. They will not stop us."

Jake had never been claustrophobic before, but the four walls closed in on him. Jake shouted. "Just let her go!"

Geoffrey chuckled. "Now why would I do that? I think you have forgotten you destroyed my life, Jake. Back then, you were the young, hotshot news reporter, fresh out of college, who did not care who you hurt. Your reporting ruined my father. I was there when my father killed himself. You probably do not even remember him. Mayor Dennis Barr."

Barr. The links fell into place. Jake remembered the investigative story he'd written. The mayor with a mistress. He'd killed the young woman. And then he'd covered it up. To avoid jail time, he'd committed suicide. No wonder Geoffrey was deranged. "I'm sorry to hear that. But your dad had an affair. He killed her, covered it up, and then committed suicide. Your dad ruined his own life." Maybe Jake could stall until help arrived.

"Nonsense. He provided for us. That woman who

died was a nobody, a mistress who threatened to talk to the other candidate. A non-entity no one would miss. But you continued to probe, ask questions. Your story went public. The police re-investigated and found more evidence, found a witness who could place my dad at the scene."

The jogger. So that's why she looked familiar.

"The police were going to arrest him, so Dad killed himself," Geoffrey continued. "And you published another story. Afterward, Mom lost it, and she sent Alli and me away to live with our kooky old grandmother. My life..." He gritted his teeth. "We went through hell after that. Did you know? Did you feel our suffering? Well, you are about to understand. You see, I am here to return the favor. Why would I kill you and end your pain when I can kill her and begin yours? No, I will keep you alive a wee bit longer."

More footsteps. Rats or a larger animal. Or maybe homeless people.

Allison cleared her throat. "Time of death?"

Jake shuddered. She hadn't seen her Dad die, so what was her excuse? Maybe losing her dad and living with a psychopathic sibling. Who knew?

"Hm?" Geoffrey asked.

"Now who's the brains?" Allison pointed at Carlotta. "She's supposed to commit suicide after she learns of his death."

Jake shook his head. Pure evil.

"Wow, Alli. I have to hand it to you this time. It is an easy fix though. Murder instead of suicide. Let me see. You will need to grab a knife from my bag. Make sure we get Jake's prints on there."

Completely maniacal. He'd reported on some weirdoes in his time but had been lucky...no, blessed, not to come so close to such characters.

Allison thumbed toward Jake. "That takes care of her, but what about him?"

"Jealous husband upset over impending divorce, finds wife with her friend. Stabs her to death. Friend stabs him as an act of self-defense, of course."

Jake's stomach churned at the thought of someone plunging a knife into his beloved. *Gotta play along, have to stall.* Jake willed his hands to stop shaking and forced a grin. "Of course."

Shadows moved in the distance.

"And we will collect some extra DNA for the road. No one need ever find Randy Rader's body, but supposing they should, I want to make sure the police can connect his death with Jake."

Jake pointed at Geoffrey. "You killed him, too."

"I planted the fake passport to keep you guessing. I knew you would show up. Good thing, too, since I removed the passport using gloves, but your fingerprints will be all over the place. I have not killed him yet. Just have him tied up for now. No, after Ed, I realized I wanted Carlotta to be my first kill." He moved closer to Carlotta. "Right?" He winked.

Jake clenched his fists. "You're sick—"

Geoffrey chuckled. "And what is your motive for killing Randy? Come on, Jake. Help me out." Geoffrey pointed the gun toward Jake and Carlotta.

Jake's mind raced. *He'll do it. Maybe not. Stay calm.*

Just play along, keep talking. "My motive…jealousy?"

Huffing, Geoffrey put the gun to his side. "Jealous of Randy? That is the best you can do? Not much of a writer, are you?"

Allison U-turned and headed toward Geoffrey's bag. She bent down and opened it.

Sweat beaded on Jake's brow. If the police didn't arrive… Allison had her back turned. Only Geoffrey guarded them. He'd have to distract him and get the gun away. Maybe he could hit him again with his flashlight. Not the best option, but perhaps the only one. Otherwise, he couldn't do much to protect Carlotta. Geoffrey would shoot him and then murder Carlotta afterward.

A scream emanated from Allison.

Someone had grabbed her. The shuffling of footsteps. Was it the police or someone else?

Geoffrey turned toward Allison, tucking his gun to his side. "Alli?"

An officer shoved Allison against a post.

Another officer came into view, stepped closer, and pointed his weapon at Geoffrey. "Up against the post. Hold still."

As the other officer cuffed Allison, Geoffrey raised his pistol. "No!" he shouted.

Jake shielded Carlotta. He'd have to try to untie her later.

"Drop your weapon, sir!" the second officer shouted.

"No." Geoffrey yelled and then lifted the gun toward his own head.

Jake hugged Carlotta pressing her head against him. She couldn't see what Geoffrey was about to do.

Two more people sprinted in from the entrance on the opposite side of the room. Detectives Hadley and Krouse? As Geoffrey spun to face them, two officers on the other side tackled him. One wrestled for the gun. In moments, Geoffrey lay on the ground. One officer cuffed him while another secured his weapon.

Jake leaned back, breathing hard, his hands on Carlotta's shoulders in a firm grip.

Detectives Hadley and Krouse approached Jake and Carlotta.

Krouse pulled out a pocketknife and cut the zipties on Carlotta's wrists. "Can you talk?" she asked gently.

"Yes…" Carlotta rubbed her wrists. "When we get out of here."

With a nod to Hadley, Krouse escorted her down the tunnel.

Hadley detained Jake. "We need to talk…"

"Yeah, I know. And same as my wife, not here."

Hadley nodded, and they followed Krouse and Carlotta.

A few minutes later, officers escorted Geoffrey and Allison outside.

Jake searched for Carlotta. He needed to hold his wife.

Carlotta twirled around toward Jake.

His gaze met hers. "It's over."

21

Carlotta savored the French vanilla cream in her morning coffee. Peppermint was her favorite, but she preferred to save it for special occasions, like the holidays.

Rosario joined her at the table and smiled.

After resting her mug, Carlotta stared at the logo on the side. Completely different from her matched set of mugs at home. Yet she couldn't criticize her sister. Rosario did the best she could. "What are you so happy about?"

"I agreed to let Pablo move back in. We're getting back together."

Carlotta hugged her sister and sat back down. "That's great. What changed your mind?"

"God." Rosario puffed out her chest. "So, have you talked to Jake?"

Lowering her gaze, Carlotta played with the mug handle. "No." Pablo was moving back in with Rosario. She'd need to find another apartment. If she got back together with Jake, it'd be for the right reasons, not just for a place to stay.

"Why haven't you talked to him?"

She shuddered. "I'm still not over everything. Geoffrey and Allison almost killed us. I've...I've been praying. Talking to God. Letting Him fill me with His Presence, answer my questions, get rid of my fears."

"God protected you. You could come to church with Pablo, Antonio, and me."

Carlotta went to the coffeemaker for a second cup. "You're different lately. Is that also because of God?"

"Not just me, Pablo, too. He's quit using drugs, and he wants to start his own business. He bought special equipment to make his own salsa. Pablo has this little garden, and he grows his own tomatoes…"

"OK. I get that. Pablo gets clean and finds God. But you and I learned about God when we were little. What's changed for you?"

"We went to church as kids, Carlotta, but we didn't *know* God. There is more to God than going to church. You can have a relationship with Him, like really know Him. Mom and Dad never taught us that. And I'm tired of the superstitions. I'm ready to trust God instead of a four-leaf clover or horseshoe."

Carlotta stared at nothing in particular. No, their parents hadn't taught them about a relationship with God. Church was more of a tradition for their family, just something you do. Carlotta headed for the bathroom. A flurry of thoughts about God and Jake overwhelmed her. She pushed them aside. It was time to get ready for work.

~*~

Later, as the afternoon sun shone through the front windows of the library, Carlotta snatched the newspaper from the current periodicals and studied the headlines.

A big write-up about Geoffrey. The coroner had ruled Ed Gorman's death as a heart attack linked to a pre-existing heart defect. Geoffrey hadn't technically killed Ed but scared the poor man to death. How sad.

She kept reading. Long ago, Geoffrey's dad, a former Cincinnati mayor, had engaged in an affair. He'd accidentally killed his mistress because she threatened to expose him, which would cost him the re-election. Then when the heat was on, he'd committed suicide in front of his son, Allen Jeffery. The atrocity Geoffrey witnessed started him down a dark path. He harmed and killed animals, which just further led him to move onto people.

Who should suffer most in Geoffrey's twisted mind but Jake, the reporter who broke the story about his dad—the one Geoffrey felt drove his dad to take his life. First, Geoffrey just wanted to kill Ed and scare Carlotta to hurt Jake, in addition to harming his marriage with the help of his sister. Then Geoffrey had gotten such a rush from meeting Carlotta, he decided to track and kill her. She shuddered.

Allison had overheard Jake talk with Randy about his upcoming trip to the retreat. Geoffrey had someone follow Jake from his home, mug him at the railroad crossing, and then later shoot him with a crossbow at the men's retreat. And why? Maybe simply to hurt Jake even more, to make him suffer. Carlotta covered her mouth. Once, she and Geoffrey had discussed the notes she'd received, and she'd even confided in him about Oliver, her ex-fiancé. Using that information, Geoffrey could harm Jake and deflect blame on Oliver. How insidious!

Jake was right. Despite being a psycho, Geoffrey really had far-reaching connections. Thankfully, none of them involved the local police. She read further into the article.

Allison drugged Jake and made it look as if he'd slept with her. Geoffrey had sent pipe bombs to the newspaper building and had sent flowers and notes to Carlotta using Jake's name and address. Geoffrey hired someone to plant drugs on Pablo and attempted to kidnap a jogger who had ID'd his dad years ago to scare her. He'd kidnapped Randy and was eventually going to kill him and Jake and her. Officers had found Randy bound and gagged, cold and hungry, not far from where Carlotta had been held in the tunnels.

She shook her head. To think that Geoffrey and his sister concocted such a plan—to drug people, plant evidence, kidnap, murder—whatever it took to accomplish their plan. Such disregard for life. And how did it all start? With bitterness. Similar to her anger toward Jake. Ouch. A flush swept across her cheeks.

Carlotta's phone buzzed. A text message notification appeared on her screen. She opened the message from Rosario.

Did you look at the newspaper yet? Turn to page 4.

Carlotta grabbed the newspaper and turned to the page.

Her boss approached. "Girl, did you read that

yet?"

She stared at Becca. "Page 4?"

Becca giggled. "Yes, page 4."

Carlotta shook her head. "I just read the stuff on the front page about Geoffrey being caught and the police catching the men behind the human trafficking ring, and how the authorities located the three missing girls. Two food truck workers were arrested, in conjunction with a larger network of traffickers. The workers would cater events, drug some of the food and drinks, and snatch women."

Becca bounced on tiptoes. "Well, hurry."

"OK, OK." Carlotta picked up the paper and took it to a nearby table. She sat, spread the paper out flat, and turned to page 4. Wait. Why was her picture there? "Carlotta is smart, feisty, kind, and...beautiful?"

"Keep going." Becca pointed to the article. "He professes his love for you. Apologizes. It's all right here."

Carlotta glanced at the byline. "Senior Editor, Jake Hartman." Then Stu must have retired. After the newspaper reinstated Jake, Stu must have rehired and promoted him. "Good for him. He got what he wanted."

"No, not everything," a man spoke from behind her.

Carlotta spun around. "Jake?"

"I don't have you. I love you. Move back in, Carlotta."

Tears filled her eyes, one escaped. She swiped it away.

Jake moved closer. "What's holding you back?"

"Just waiting for you to ask."

Jake embraced her, and she relaxed into his arms.

Becca turned to walk away. "I'll leave you two alone." She gave a thumbs up as she exited.

"I have one more assignment before I get back to work. Stu's got me on a short leash until he clears out his things. His last day is Friday." Jake chuckled.

Carlotta gazed without focus. "Oh. Can I help you with research?"

"If that's what you want to call it, baby."

She leaned closer. "And what are you researching exactly?"

"It's an article on the finer points of smooching and canoodling."

Carlotta narrowed her gaze. "Kissing?"

"Yeah, can you help me out? They say write what you know!" He shrugged, leaning in.

Her lips connected with Jake's. A tingling sensation swept up the back of her neck and across her face. Jake pulled back. Carlotta inhaled a deep breath. Her knees grew weak. "I...I um..."

He stepped closer, whispered in her ear. "I'll need a lot more help later. Do you think you and I could stop by Rosario's after work, grab your things, go back to our house, and do more research?"

Lightheaded, Carlotta coughed. "I get the feeling this wasn't Stu's assignment."

He shrugged and stared into her eyes, barely blinking. "So, about that research request?"

Carlotta shuffled her feet. "Yes, tonight."

Jake bowed but caught her gaze as he straightened his posture. "You've been very helpful with my research, Miss Librarian."

22

In her own home, Carlotta rolled back and forth beneath the duvet but couldn't find a comfortable position in her bed. Might as well get up. The alternating gurgling and dripping noises of the coffee machine kept her awake. And yet she didn't mind. The familiar sounds welcomed her. She was back home with Jake.

And not because she'd fixed him or rescued him, not because she could control him. But because Jake had changed.

He wasn't the only one. She cast a glance at the journal on the nightstand. It sat atop the book her counselor had recommended and a new Bible she'd purchased. So many feelings had flooded her mind lately, ones she wasn't aware of—with this new awareness, her migraines disappeared. Even her stomach improved. She'd gone a month without restocking the pantry with the pink stuff or antacids.

And God. She'd changed her entire view on Him. In the past, Carlotta had taken her view of her earthly mother and father and how they had treated her and projected that imperfect relationship model onto a perfect God. *No wonder I had trouble trusting Him before.*

Carlotta blew out a breath. Grace. Whew, what a

completely new concept for both her and Jake. The new feeling was strangely warm and welcoming, and yet foreign at the same time. Peace replaced overwhelming frustration.

Jake didn't have to be her knight in shining armor. Carlotta already had a Savior, a Rescuer, Redeemer, and Friend—one she could depend upon and trust to meet all her needs. She sat up in her bed. *I don't need to be in control. How prideful to think I can do it all on my own.*

God was in control, not her, and she could rest easy in that assurance. A long journey to recovery lay ahead. Jake gave her control of the finances, attended gambling addiction meetings, and met with Pastor Clyde for Bible study. She met with a counselor and attended a ladies' Bible study with Rosario. Jake worked on his own problems while she worked on hers. Yet they weren't alone. Their love for God and each other united them, encouraging one another.

More and more, she understood what Pablo said about finding his worth in the person of Jesus Christ. For so long, Carlotta had put her worth in the fleeting things of life—her job, her marriage, her ability to have children—all things that could change. Now, she found her hope in Christ and the salvation He provided— something that wouldn't change.

Carlotta swung her feet over the side of the bed and planted them on the floor. Where was Jake?

She tiptoed downstairs and eyed a crumpled blanket on the couch where Jake had spent the night with Gracie snuggled beside him. Carlotta was back in the house with Jake, and yet, intimacy was still awkward.

Most couples made love and had babies. But she and Jake...nothing fruitful came from their efforts. It was why sex had become so emotionless. It was all about the end product. Could they conceive or couldn't they? And yet in these past few months, the expectation faded away. No doctors. No needles. Could they regain the passion they'd lost?

Jake wandered over and handed her a coffee mug. His gaze traveled the length of her body and lingered longer than usual.

Carlotta took in a deep breath and sat down the mug. She retrieved an envelope from the counter and handed it to Jake. She bit her lip and then folded her arms against herself. Her silk nightgown felt cold against her skin as she waited.

An ashen look spread across Jake's face as he raised the envelope. "What is this, Carlotta? The divorce papers?"

Carlotta took a step closer and rested one hand on Jake's chest. She raised her gaze to meet his. "I think we both know what to do with them."

His face regained composure. "I have just the thing." He opened a kitchen drawer and retrieved a lighter.

Carlotta touched his arm. "Wait. Before you do that, you must promise me something."

Jake's eyes sparkled. "Anything."

She grabbed his other arm and pulled him closer. "That we'll continue to go to counseling both alone and together. We owe it to our marriage."

He nodded and then leaned in for a kiss.

She savored the taste of his lips and hesitated to pull away. Lightheaded, she stopped to take a breath. "Now about those papers...."

Jake laughed. "What? Oh, those papers. Yes, let's take care of those." He gripped his lighter and the paperwork.

Carlotta reached out and grabbed his arm. "Maybe later?" She gave him her best come-hither look and batted her eyelashes.

Jake quirked a brow. "Later?"

Giggling, Carlotta raced for the stairs.

~*~

The warmth inside Krohn Conservatory provided a stark contrast with the crisp fall weather outside, a bit cooler than the seasonal average. Bright fall foliage had started to litter the city sidewalks outside, and though vibrant, proved no match for the exotic species featured inside. Jake admired the various rare and unusual plants as he rambled along the pathway with Carlotta as his guide. It was a perk of having a spouse who'd volunteered at many places within the city over the years. Carlotta had picked up a breadth of knowledge on a variety of topics. She knew the insides and outsides of many locations within the city.

She spouted off a fact about another plant species and then stared at him. Her eyes sparkled as she babbled.

Heat radiated through Jake's body. *I've never understood why she volunteers all the time and even chided her for it. But now, I get it. She loves what she does, and it fills a void. One I wish I'd filled more often. But even I can't meet all her needs. Only God Himself can do that. Still, I want to try harder, take an interest in her hobbies, and spend more time together—fall in love all over again. If she'll let me.*

Carlotta stepped forward to point out another species, but he grabbed her arm, pulling her close. He focused on the coat she'd chosen to wear. The green one he'd bought her for her birthday.

He met her gaze and placed his hands on her shoulders. "So maybe we can't have biological children. Let's build a family...together. You know, we've never talked about my dad. His death was painful for me. But I need to explain something. When my grandmother was pregnant with my dad, she lost her husband. Everyone told her, 'Get rid of the baby. Here, try this herb.' She refused, even when her pregnancy got rough, and she became very ill. She gave birth to my dad. Without him, I wouldn't be here. I haven't always been a firm believer in the existence of God, but I guess I've always felt like adoption was important. There are kids who need homes. And I've been talking to Detective Krouse—"

She tilted her head.

Jake lifted his hands in a defensive posture. "All purely professional—and she said there are many sibling groups who need someone to foster or adopt them. And about dogs, I never said I hated them. You assumed. I had a terrific dog as a kid. Had him for many years. But then he died. I didn't want to go through that again."

"What about Gracie?"

He shrugged. "She'll adjust."

Carlotta lowered her gaze.

Jake rubbed the back of his neck. Had he said the wrong thing?

Carlotta peered at him. "Do you mean all of that, or are you saying what you think I want to hear?"

He grabbed her hand and continued to walk to the next group of plants. He did a double take of the area. Purple and white orchids framed the space. As good a place as any. "I'm serious, but..." Maybe he was pushing things too fast. Perhaps she needed more time.

Carlotta groaned. "But what?"

"We need to renew our vows first. I want to start things off right before children arrive. I'm the one who chose to go out with Allison that night, and I need to make that right." Jake dropped to one knee. He pulled out an engagement ring. "Carlotta, will you marry me?" He cleared his throat. "Again?"

She nodded. "For better or worse."

"We've had our share of the worse, haven't we?" He winked.

"And God got us through that."

"Yeah, He did." Jake put the ring on Carlotta's finger and kissed her. Short, but still very sweet. Then he grabbed her hand and continued to walk along the conservatory path. "So, we haven't talked about the number of kids. I was thinking five boys. You know, like our own basketball team."

Carlotta's eyes widened. "What? No girls?"

"I guess we need a cheerleader. Wow. Six kids. I better get a second job." He chuckled.

~*~

Jake admired the dome-shaped roof of the Cincinnati Observatory. His toe cramped, and his gaze shifted to the dress shoes he'd found at the back of his closet. Good thing he didn't have a reason to wear them more often. Still, what a reason. A good one. And another occasion for which to be thankful. Presently, he didn't find himself to be as nervous as the last time he'd worn them. The florist had arranged white flowers inside white vases strategically placed in front of the posts at the bottom of the stairs leading to the observatory. As usual, Carlotta was right. Mount Lookout was the perfect place to host the event. *Thank You, God, for the warmer weather today.*

He stole a glance at the guests. Both completely off-duty, Detective Hadley wore a plaid shirt and sat next to Detective Krouse. Good thing Stu and his wife were seated in the opposite aisle. Randy relaxed next to Becca and snorted. Probably sharing notes about conspiracy theories, ghost stories, or comic heroes.

Pablo tapped him on the shoulder.

"Hey, best man. What's up?"

His brother-in-law handed him a jar.

Jake examined it. Tomato-red chunky salsa. "Is this what I think it is?"

Pablo nodded. "A prototype I'm taking to a friend, Todd Woodward."

Why did that name sound familiar? Oh, yeah. "The guy who opened the trendy new grocery store in Oakley?"

"Yep. He's thinking of featuring P and R salsa in his stores."

"P and R?" Jake chuckled. "Oh, I get it. Pablo and Rosie. Nice."

"Not only that, I've been working on a hot sauce formula. Todd wants to market it to restaurants. Said they might have to use special packaging, though. That stuff is so spicy."

Jake stared at nothing in particular.

"What is it?"

Jake shook his head and set the salsa on the ground. He shook Pablo's hand. "Thanks for the salsa."

"You're welcome. Are you sure everything is OK? You're not having second thoughts, are you?"

"Nope. Just thinking about what you said. About the hot sauce. So spicy you have to contain it just right. Otherwise, it can really mess things up. Just like grudges and unforgiving attitudes. Boy, am I glad Carlotta has forgiven me."

"And that Jesus forgave us?"

Jake nodded. Geoffrey was bitter, but he'd chosen revenge. Carlotta, instead, had chosen love and forgiveness.

The processional played. Antonio skipped down the center aisle, carrying rings tied on a pillow. Rosario followed behind.

Jake pulled at his collar and then glanced at his bride as she strode toward him. That smile. So much for any nervousness.

Antonio and his mom stood off to the left, Pablo to the right.

Carlotta approached and stood by his side.

"Dearly beloved," Pastor Clyde began.

Something else was different about this ceremony. Not quite as long as the first.

Pastor Clyde cleared his throat. "You may kiss the bride."

A beaming expression overtook Carlotta. Jake moved in closer and gazed at her. His pulse raced, his lips parted, and he embraced his wife. Carlotta moistened her lips and wrapped her arms around him. As their lips touched, an electrical jolt traveled the length of his body. He didn't want the moment to end.

Carlotta pulled away. Her cheeks glowed.

Jake and Carlotta turned to face the guests. He took her hand in his and lightly clasped it. "Thank you for this rewrite, this do-over."

She returned the squeeze. "I couldn't think of a better man for the job."

EPILOGUE

Carlotta smiled. Pink tubular blossoms covered Elizabeth, the Christmas cactus. The plant set equidistant between the sink and the window. Not too much light. Not too little light. Just enough. Carlotta touched her throat. The form of another Christmas cactus, one with purple flowers, peeked out from behind Elizabeth. Who was this? Bending closer, Carlotta studied the plant. A note had been taped to the side of the flower pot. Jake's handwriting adorned the side. Carlotta chuckled. Mr. Darcy. Who else, right?

As Carlotta walked away from the plants, she shifted her gaze to the puppy calendar. A year? How could it have already been that long? Then again, it added up: six months for her and Jake to complete foster care training and the daunting tasks involved in an adoption home study for the county, and six months since five-year-old Marta had been placed in their home. But it was worth it. All the time and effort, all the measures the county required, ensuring safe homes for the foster children.

She grabbed her hunter green, down winter coat and headed toward the front door. A red and green festive holiday doorknob hanger with jingle bells garnished the drab brass knob. Carlotta opened the door and stooped down to retrieve the newspaper from the front porch. After scanning the thin layer of snow covering the ground, which rapidly expanded, she re-opened the door and stepped inside. She took one last glance out the window. Though clouds spanned the sky, a faint glimmer of the sun shone through.

Footsteps sounded from the other end of the hallway. Her gaze shifted to her husband. She put her hand to her mouth to suppress a chuckle. "I see you like the Christmas sweater your Aunt Edna sent you."

Jake winked. "Who doesn't love fuzzy sweaters with gingerbread men on them?" One hand behind his back, he smooched her and then handed her a bright, colorful bouquet of mixed flowers—red, pink, yellow, and white. "These are for you. Nothing bad. Good news, actually."

Carlotta located a vase and added the flowers, along with some water.

Jake followed her.

"Did you get a new job?"

"Even better. Our caseworker called. The biological parents have terminated their rights. Carol said we should meet with her on Friday to discuss more details regarding adopting Marta."

"Can this be happening?" Carlotta swiped a tear.

Jake placed his hands on her shoulders. "Are you OK?"

She nodded and maintained an unfocused stare. "I really hoped the county could reunite Marta with her parents if possible. I wanted them to love Marta as we love her. She deserves to be loved by everyone."

"We both did. But since that wasn't possible, I'm so glad we have the chance to welcome her into our family, permanently."

"Me, too."

Jake glanced at the grandfather clock. "It's 8:00 AM. Shouldn't Marta be up by now?" He and Carlotta jogged upstairs and then down the hall to Marta's room. Two shades of pink paint and various pretty pony decals adorned the walls of the five-year-old's bedroom.

Carlotta gently laid a hand on little Marta's shoulder. The girl lay nestled all snug beneath her pony comforter in her pink bed. Gracie lay at the end of the bed. "Marta, wake up. It's Christmas morning."

Marta rolled over. A glum expression washed over the child. No matter what her biological parents had done, they were still a part of Marta's story.

The social worker had warned them the holidays could be difficult for children who'd grown up in foster care. Had she received presents in the past or even celebrated Christmas at all? Carlotta kneeled down next to the bed and met Marta's gaze. "Let's go downstairs." Carlotta stood.

Marta joined her and stepped into pink fuzzy bunny slippers next to the bed.

Carlotta and Jake each held one of Marta's tiny hands, led her downstairs, and reclined with her on the couch—Marta nestled in the middle with Jake and Carlotta on either side. Colorful lights twinkled on the Christmas tree. Gracie batted at low-hanging ornaments. Light snow fell outside. The fresh fragrance of pine permeated the air.

Jake belted out *Joy to the World* in a falsetto voice.

Marta giggled and then hummed along.

A smile spread across Carlotta's face, and she harmonized with them. Her shoulders relaxed. The happy family she had always hoped for was finally a reality. Not in her way or in her timing, but in God's. Love filled her home and their lives.

A Devotional Moment

Looking diligently lest any man fail of the grace of God; lest any root of bitterness springing up trouble you, and thereby many be defiled... Hebrews 12:15

Sometimes, it's hard to forgive someone when they've done something that results in feelings of betrayal and anguish. What is done cannot be undone, and there is a hopelessness attached to the betrayal that can make a person bitter and sad. Jesus preaches that we must forgive for the sake of our own souls. We have to find Him within us, ask for His strength, and give the other person compassion and grace for what they've done. A hard task, yet still a task our Saviour willingly did for us.

In **Hold for Release**, the protagonist is seeking answers to the bitterness in her heart. In the midst of her own anguish, the people around her accidentally get involved in a deadly game of deceit and danger that threatens her own life. In the midst of sorrowful brokenness, God works to help all involved and thereby, the protagonist can truly claim beauty for ashes.

Do you find it difficult to let go of feelings of

betrayal and anguish, or any other negative emotion attached to things that others have done to you? Forgiving someone isn't always easy. It often feels unfair. But God commands you to forgive in the same way He's forgiven you in the past and will do in the future whenever you sincerely ask for forgiveness.

Remember, that when you don't forgive, the only person you hurt is yourself. Unforgiveness breeds bitterness, and bitterness is the stuff of which bad decisions are made. No matter what someone has done to offend you, hurt you—even if it's something unforgivable—forgive them. Daily, if that's what it takes. Forgiveness isn't a feeling, isn't an emotion, it's an act of the will, and you can do it…and when you do it, you'll be more happy and less stressed than you can ever be by holding on to your bitterness, hurt and anger.

LORD, WHEN I AM WEAK, WHEN I AM BITTER AND ANGRY AT ANOTHER PERSON, HELP ME TO RISE TO YOU, TO GATHER YOUR COMPASSION AND MERCY INTO MY HEART SO THAT I MAY FORGIVE. TAKE THE BROKENNESS FROM ME, AND HELP ME TO BE STRONGER AND EVER FAITHFUL TO YOU. IN JESUS' NAME I PRAY, AMEN.

Thank you…

for purchasing this Harbourlight title. For other inspirational stories, please visit our on-line bookstore at www.pelicanbookgroup.com.

For questions or more information, contact us at customer@pelicanbookgroup.com.

Harbourlight Books
The Beacon in Christian Fiction™
an imprint of Pelican Book Group
www.pelicanbookgroup.com

Connect with Us
www.facebook.com/Pelicanbookgroup
www.twitter.com/pelicanbookgrp

To receive news and specials, subscribe to our bulletin
http://pelink.us/bulletin

May God's glory shine through
this inspirational work of fiction.

AMDG

You Can Help!

At Pelican Book Group it is our mission to entertain readers with fiction that uplifts the Gospel. It is our privilege to spend time with you awhile as you read our stories.

We believe you can help us to bring Christ into the lives of people across the globe. And you don't have to open your wallet or even leave your house!

Here are 3 simple things you can do to help us bring illuminating fiction™ to people everywhere.

1) If you enjoyed this book, write a positive review. Post it at online retailers and websites where readers gather. And share your review with us at reviews@pelicanbookgroup.com (this does give us permission to reprint your review in whole or in part.)

2) If you enjoyed this book, recommend it to a friend in person, at a book club or on social media.

3) If you have suggestions on how we can improve or expand our selection, let us know. We value your opinion. Use the contact form on our web site or e-mail us at customer@pelicanbookgroup.com

God Can Help!

Are you in need? The Almighty can do great things for you. Holy is His Name! He has mercy in every generation. He can lift up the lowly and accomplish all things. Reach out today.

Do not fear: I am with you; do not be anxious: I am your God. I will strengthen you, I will help you, I will uphold you with my victorious right hand.
                                        ~Isaiah 41:10 (NAB)

We pray daily, and we especially pray for everyone connected to Pelican Book Group—that includes you! If you have a specific need, we welcome the opportunity to pray for you. Share your needs or praise reports at http://pelink.us/pray4us

Free eBook Offer

We're looking for booklovers like you to partner with us! Join our team of influencers today and periodically receive free eBooks!

For more information
Visit http://pelicanbookgroup.com/booklovers

How About Free Audiobooks?

We're looking for audiobook lovers, too! Partner with us as an audiobook lover and periodically receive free audiobooks!

For more information
Visit
http://pelicanbookgroup.com/booklovers/freeaudio.html

or e-mail
booklovers@pelicanbookgroup.com